EXCLUSIVE LOVE

BLAZIN' LOVE BOOK THREE

JA'NESE DIXON

PUBLISHING

ISBN-13: 978-1-950405-04-6 (paperback)

Printed in the United States of America.

CONTENTS

His sweet chocolate kisses are off limits!

It's Easter Sunday.

I'm sitting on the pew next to my Mom, handling my daughter duties when HE—Darius Grant— walks in sparking thoughts that guarantee I'm going straight to hell with gasoline panties on.

I'm Charlee Stuart. I've joined my best friends in starting an elite concierge service. My assignment is to find premium services for our upscale clientele. Truth is, I have no idea what I'm doing, but I won't fail my guys.

He takes the seat in front of me blocking my view. At six foot, fine, and filthy rich, I'm hoping I won't be struck by lightning. Then I remember Darius is off limits. But his chocolates may be just what I need to test my skills of persuasion.

I'm not the kind of woman to chase a dude, but I might hop in his direction. And I'm making a promise on this hard-ass pew before the Man and my momma, that I will not...will not fall for Darius again.

Then he turns and winks in my direction. For the love of things hot and tempting, please...

Father...take me now!

"$\mathcal{M}$y mamma's gonna kill me."

I'm driving through the streets of Austin on two of my four wheels, using every ounce of power in my V8 engine. There's a yellow light between the church and me and I consider running it when by instinct I slam on my breaks.

"Sorry." I wave a hand, scaring a little old lady and myself. She flips the bird, and I don't have time to be offended. I hook a right and circle the block, swooping my sports car in the first available space.

Today, I'm thankful for Daddy's guilt gift. I made it across town in half the ETA thanks to heavy foot and my Audi jumping at the chance to show out. I hop out then realize I forgot something, "My Bible."

I run back and grab my childhood bible from the door. I'm not a regular church attendee, but I know the black girl rules.

We always, *always* attend church at least three times a year. Mother's Day, Easter, and Christmas. Those three days keep me in my mother's and aunt's good graces, and I can skip a few spaces on the prayer list when life seems unfair, and I need a little grace, like today.

I try to run, but it's more of a shuffle up the sidewalk. My pencil skirt won't allow much movement. I enter the air-conditioned building brushing my sweaty hair to the side and plopping my wide-brimmed Sunday hat on my head.

I grab a program from the usher rolling her eyes at me and use it to fan my face. Like I don't know I'm late. *Whatever.*

I peak at the mirror in the little bathroom and gasp at the sight. I need to do some damage control. I run in grabbing a handful of tissue, drying the sweat. I glance up and send up a prayer.

"Lord I promise to stop leaving at the last minute if you don't let my momma cuss me out for being late."

I'm exaggerating. My mother won't really cuss me out. But her eyes will no doubt make up for what her mouth won't say.

I glance through the diamond window on the old wood swinging doors that lead to the sanctuary. I'm searching for her, and of course, she's on the third row sitting near the center aisle.

I see my guys a few rows back from my mother, and there's an empty seat on the end. *Praise God*, the fifth row it is. I tip-toe inside on the balls of my feet trying to keep the click of my heels to a minimum. I make it to the end of pew and Taylor picks up the purse she had holding my seat.

"Thank you," I whisper, dropping to the hard wood.

"You'd be late to your own funeral." She whispers laughing behind the church fan.

"Hush." I pull at the hem of my skirt and take a deep sigh of relief, maybe momma didn't notice.

"Charlee." I glance towards the harsh tone. *Or maybe not*. She gives a not so discreet nod to the empty space beside her. I roll my eyes, in my head, cause, I ain't crazy. I look down the pew and Hunter, Harper, Chase, and Taylor are laughing. I can't hear it, but the shake of their shoulders is proof enough.

"I can't stand y'all—"

"Charlee Raine—" Now she's hissing my middle name. I stand and leave a perfectly good seat. Thankfully the choir is moving to the front so my seat switch won't draw too much attention until I have to scoot pass a million people to get to my mother.

"Excuse me...excuse me...pardon me...." I drop with an unladylike thud next to my mother.

"I guess I know what I need to get you for Christmas." My mother says without moving her lips.

"What?"

"A watch." My head snaps in her direction.

"Ha ha Ma." I kiss her cheek and wiggle to get

comfortable. I glance over my shoulder to see the guys still laughing. I stick out my tongue like we did as kids and Chase is trying to cover her laughter with a cough.

"Charlee Raine Stuart."

"Yes, ma'am."

I turn as the choir director motions for the choir to stand in unison, and I lean closer to my mother to enjoy the Easter morning service.

An hour in and I'm glad I didn't miss the children speeches. They laugh, cry, and have to be pulled off the stage for freezing. Then Pastor Dillard stands behind the pulpit.

"Show the babies some love y'all." The audience claps and shouts to encourage the children as they walk out the sanctuary in a single-file line. "Before we get to this morning's message I want to bring up a very special member of Agape Love's family. Darius Grant, will you join me?" Pastor Dillard gestures to the stage and the congregation claps. "He's one of our own. Y'all can do better than that."

My mother digs an elbow into my side. Still clapping with the rest of the members. But I can't take my eyes off the man walking to the front. I haven't seen him since he walked out of my life to travel the world. He said he wanted to learn from the best of the best. And his plans didn't include me.

Darius throws up a hand acknowledging the applause he's receiving, and then his eyes settle on mine. I glance down at my hands not trusting myself and my lingering feelings for him. I'm liable to kiss him or kick him in the nuts.

What is he doing here? I can hear the whispers around me. No doubt the mothers are sending smoke signals to their daughters because Darius stands close to six feet and is finer than frog hair. His custom suit shows off his broad shoulders and lean body. He has a confident swagger, and he's part of the beard gang, and it looks good on him.

I cross my legs a little tighter. Scooting over a little from my mother because I can't have lightning striking us both down for the thoughts going through my head. Because the look in his eyes says, he's thinking what I'm thinking. And I shouldn't be thinking what I'm thinking in the Lord's house.

I look at the fan covered ceiling praying for relief and a plan of escape.

"Brother Darius. I hear you're thinking about returning home."

I glance back at the pulpit.

"Yes, sir I am." He smiles, and I swear a collective sigh rings across the sanctuary. "I am here meeting with some people about relocating Delicious Chocolates headquarters to Austin, TX."

The audience claps.

"This will mean jobs." Pastor Dillard confirms.

"Yes, sir." There's more clapping and women standing to their feet, waving handkerchiefs towards him. I snort.

I glance over my shoulder at the guys and roll my

eyes good and hard this time. Harper gives a sympathetic shrug.

"And we hope opportunities to partner with people right here in my own community," Darius says.

My spidey sense kicks in. I look back at Hunter giving her my best, *Did you hear that?* look. She tosses a *Go gettum* smirk, and Mr. Darius Grant is more than a fine man in a suit. He just might be the answer to my prayers.

My guys aren't just my guys, but they are my sisters, my best friends, and my business partners. Hunter started Platinum Privilege, an elite concierge service, and we all hold a percentage. Hunter and her husband Ben carry the heaviest load, handling the day to day operations, contract negotiations, and such. And the rest of us—Harper, Parker, Chase, Taylor, Payton, Alex, Ryann, Jordan, and I—supply our family connections, funding, and social juice.

I'm still fumbling around when it comes to the business part. But I love when we get dressed in our Men in Black suits—dubbed GIB, *Guys in Black*—and watch heads turn in awe of ten fine-ass black women strolling like the bosses we are.

I cringe, I probably shouldn't use the word ass in church. I'll blame it on my higher than normal stress levels.

Hunter started passing out assignments for each of us to handle before she has the babies. Mine is to find a couple of premium services for our upscale clients, and I'm failing, *big time*.

I never thought trying to persuade business owners to work with us would be so damn hard. I did it again. I smack my head and shake the curse words from my mind. I need to ask the Man for a hand, and I can't do it with a potty mouth—as my mother would call it. I look back towards the men and listen intently.

"I always thought he'd be my son-in-law," Mamma whispers.

"Don't Ma."

I can't entertain those types of thoughts because Darius Grant is off limits.

I've been there, done that, and my body and heart can tell the tale. He's the man that knows all my secrets. The man I can't use a fake smile to hide my insecurities. The man who proved, like my father, that men like him don't stick around.

Not for the long haul.

So, Darius in all his finest can't come near my heart, but he may be precisely what I need to get my boss-lady feet wet.

I need to prove to myself and the guys that I can hold my own in the partnership. That I'm more than a good laugh and the life of the party—although I'm those things too. And who knows, maybe this will be the opportunity I need to start a new career for myself instead of working for the family business when needed and collecting my inheritance.

I roll my shoulders back and listen for any other clues I need to get some alone time with Darius to discuss Delicious Chocolates. We are a local business, and we once were friends. I'm confident I can't convince him to work with us.

My mother jabs me in the side again as Darius heads towards us. Then he enters the pew in front us with more grace than I could muster. People turn and stand as he approaches. He nods showing his pearly whites, but his eyes never stray too far from mine. Then he stops at the seat directly in front of me.

"Hello, Mrs. Stuart."

"Hey, baby." My mother says as if he's not a full grown-ass man.

"Charlee."

"Darius." The heat in his eyes is a downright sin. Heat starts in my gut and burst through my body. I can't stop it, and the cocky smile on his face tells me he knows it. "Stop." I hiss.

"Yes, ma'am Charlee Raine." He moves to turn back to the front but not before tossing a wink my way. Then I see the back of his head.

"You need to bag that one baby." My mother whispers for my ears to hear.

"Mamma, did you just say bag?" I ask as we stand to hear the scripture read.

"Ain't that how y'all young folks say it?" She winks over her shoulder, turning back to the front.

I shake my head. I can't deal with her. I close my eyes taking several deep breaths. I have a private meeting with my mind, heart, and woman parts. *We cannot, will not get sucked into Darius Grant's clutches. Amen.* I add for good measure because I need all the help I can get.

CHAPTER 2

DARIUS

"**S**on, me and your mother, go way back." Her hand slinks up and down my arm.

I hold back a cringe, releasing her hand. Then I take a step back.

This must be the new season of The Bachelor. I shake hands and pass out business cards. I hear about kids graduating from college, and I'm extended several forceful dinner offers, like this one.

"Helen, I haven't seen you in forever." My mother appears like an angel, and I kiss her cheek. "You better get moving boy because you know this one ain't wrap too tight." She mumbles, and it takes a higher power to keep from laughing.

Pastor Dillard's enthusiasm makes me excited about moving Delicious Chocolate home. But business isn't my only reason for returning.

My quest to make something of myself and build my

business made the world my home. But no one replaces my mother and the woman I left behind. It took traveling to exotic places and seeing the best the world has to offer to determine that there was something...better yet someone missing. And for all of my entrepreneur ambition, one woman has the power to make me stay.

Charlee.

The thought of finding love playing dodge ball is hilarious. I called her Charlie Brown, and she planted a basketball smack in my face. I gathered my bleeding nose in my hands and glared at the crazy girl with fire in her eyes. "I bet you won't say that again," was her retort with a hand on her hip. I thought she broke my nose and after going to the principal's office and serving detention for a week, I knew that she was my woman.

I chuckle at the thought of her discomfort this morning. I can only imagine the smart remarks running through her head.

I knew I'd see her this morning in church, yet I was unprepared for the feelings she's unleashed. I keep on ear on the conversation between my mother and Miss Helen as I search the crowd.

The service closed a half hour ago, but most of the congregation is hanging out on the lawn waiting for the kids to finish with the Easter egg hunt. The sea of people is finely dressed. Women in an array of spring pinks, yellows, and mint greens. Men in suits and ties. The smell of fried fish lingers in the air. The robust sound of talking and laughter puts a smile on my face.

Then I feel a tinkling sensation. I glance over my shoulder, and a stunning group of women is heading in my direction. Most of the faces are familiar. I sweep their group until I land on the woman who has seared herself to my soul and secured a leash to my heart.

Charlee Raine Stuart.

I feel a hand embrace my forearm and I glance towards my mother. She knows. She knows what this moment means to me. How I left needing to prove myself and I'm returning a better version of myself, but I want more.

It might be selfish. But my gut tells me my more is wrapped up in the woman that had a legion of soldiers guarding her heart. I clench a fist at my side a few times to relieve the tension mounting in my chest.

Today, Charlee's wearing a mustard yellow body contouring dress. The slight tilt of her wide brim Sunday hat gives her eyes an alluring appearance and put her full lips on display.

She's talking with her friends. I let my eyes get a full drink. She's never been tall, but the high heels place her near chin height. She's what I'd call slim thick, and she carries her thickness in all the right places. My hands ache to caress her curves, and I know it's only a matter of time.

"Helen, excuse us for a moment." I hear my mother say. Then she pulls me aside, but I'm locked in a major stare down with Charlee.

"Boy, I need you to take it down several notches." My

eyes drop to hers. The smile on her face does not mask the concern in her eyes. "You are standing on the church lawn, and Pastor Dillard nor Valerie will appreciate the thoughts running through that mind of yours."

"Everybody loves chocolate." I sweep a quick glance at Charlee. The hue of her skin haunted my dreams, rich and deep like the highest grade of chocolate.

"Chocolate my tush." She chuckles. "Take it easy lover boy or Charlee will chew you up and spit you out."

"I'm cool Mamma. " I hear the shift in her voice, and I look down at her. Janice Reed is a knockout. I'm biased because she's my mother but she looks young enough to be my sister, and I know my distance hurt her. We were always the two peas in a pod, and I left home with a point to prove.

"Just take it easy. I love Charlee and Valerie, but I'd hurt somebody over you." I wrap my arms around the First Lady in my life.

"Are you good with this Ma?"

"If it means you'll stop running and come home. I'll be your wing woman." We laugh, as I cradle my mother to my heart. There's nothing I won't do for this woman.

"I'm gonna hold you to it. Because something tells me all hands will need to be on deck for this mission."

I glance back at Charlee taking a deep breath. I'm not the boy I was when I left Austin. I thought leaving home would help me get over Charlee, but the feelings I had didn't fade, they intensified. I'm not foolish enough to believe she'll fall at my feet or even wrap her arms around me. Nah, not my Charlee. She is tough as nails. But beneath her walls of steel is an unmatched heart.

"Both of y'all were kids. But handle her with care. There's nothing like having your love discarded."

"But Mom, she's the one who said leave." My eyes swing back to my mother. A simmer of frustration surfacing.

"Baby listen to me. Hurt women speak a different language. Her leave meant stay." She places a soft hand over my heart. "You can't think of this as a business transaction. You can't think you'll win her over with your looks or charm or money. That will not impress her."

"Then what Ma?"

"Time will tell. But if you leave again, you might as well kiss your second chance goodbye, *if* she gives it to you. Because judging by the look in her father's eyes, you better man up."

I follow the direction of my mother's gaze. And sure enough, I see Charles Stewart over Charlee's shoulder. "Who's that?" I ask of the young woman clinging to his arm.

"Wife number three."

Huh. "And how's Miss Valerie handling it?"

She shrugs, "Like we all do when we find ourselves replaced by a newer, younger model, she's moving on." My mother lightly pats my shoulder, and I hear the hurt in her voice. "I'll see you at the house."

"Be ready at *three* for brunch." I watch the clouds leave her eyes.

"Boy, you can't rush perfection." She winks, and sashay's off.

I shake my head as she walks towards another crowd of people. I turn back to see Charlee and her she-gang heading in my direction.

Well, well, well, what do we have here.

There's a hint of determination in her eyes.

I recognize Hunter, Harper, Taylor, and a few of the other faces. I can't recall their names. But in school, they moved in a different circle. A circle I wasn't privy to...*then*.

I face them eager to see what they're cooking up. Because no doubt they are up to *something*. It just might be the leverage I need to get what I want, and that's to prove Charlee and I belong together.

This might be the greatest challenge of my life. That's why it took me so long to return. I had to establish myself and show her all she needs is me.

I quiet the soft whisper in the corner of my mind. The thought of her saying no is real yet unfathomable. Not after all I've done and all we've endured.

I take a deep breath and search for the resolve that I need to start this war. Because what she thinks is dead is about to be resurrected.

The group closes in, and Charlee steps forward.

"Charlee Raine, to what do I owe this honor?"

CHAPTER 3

CHARLEE

*D*arius' eyes are working overtime. I knew I was in trouble the moment he turned around in the pew and whispered, "Charlee Raine."

Yes, it's my name. But it's the way he says it. The tone, the twang, the history.

After service, I huddle with the guys, as he smiles and cheeses like he's running for president.

We chat for a while when I see the window of opportunity. It feels like now or never. I head in his direction with my guys in tow. I wish we had a videographer to capture us.

We're decked out in our Easter outfits. Not as nice as our GIB suits, however, this could easily be mistaken for one of those elaborate photo shoots.

The five of us, covered in designer labels, faces beat to capacity. I'm thankful my hat is covering my earlier fiasco. My hat more than makes up for my sweaty entrance, as my spiral curls cascade down my back.

The verdict of our little guy pow-wow is, I'm up, and Darius and his chocolates are my targets.

That decision makes this runway display all business. Apparently, Harper is handling our need for getting an airplane, and Taylor is designing a custom database for our in house needs. Plus or minus a few technical glitches.

I'm scared shitless. And I can't tell them or let him know.

Not because I'm batting 100 right now. Not because I doubt my ability to get the hang of this pitching thing. It's because I know this man, as much, if not more than he knows me. Because this is the one man that I actually believed and he made me out to be a lie. But the soft smile lingering on the corners of his tempting mouth make me want to increase the security around my heart.

"Are you sure about this?" Harper asks. I feel her hand on my arm, and I look over at her trying to calm the butterfly stampede in my stomach. Then I feel Hunter close into my side.

"Hell yeah, I got this," I say, calling on all of my black-girl magic to make this happen because it's too late to take back the plan. I glance around seeing kids return from the Easter egg hunt. *Move Charlee*, I tell my feet. The crunch of the gravel beneath my heels underscore my walk to the bad side.

Okay, I'm extra dramatic. But the laser focus of his

eyes sweep my body boldly, and I'm on display. And I'm conscious of the fit of my dress, conscious of the height of my heels, conscious of how I like the response I'm getting from him.

What the fu—

I choke the thought because I will *not* say or think another swear word until I get back to my car. *Amen.*

I stop in front of Darius. We take a minute to assess each other up close.

"Charlee Raine, to what do I owe this honor?"

I extend a hand. "Long time no see."

"Oh, so we're at the handshake stage?" He stares at my offer as if offended. Then he grabs my hand and brings it to his lips.

"You do know we're in front of a church?" I tease.

"I'm sure this soft peck on your hand doesn't compare to the thoughts running through that head of yours."

I laugh. "You got me."

"How many times did you curse?"

"I will not answer that question." I chuckle.

"Give me a hug Charlee Raine."

And like old times I fall into his chest. His arms slip around my waist, not intimately, but worse, it's the type of hug that makes you body remember old times. He held me like this when my parents told me about their divorce. He held me like this when I was asked to participate in my father's wedding to his second wife, months after my parents' divorce was final. And like before, I smell the hint of his aftershave mixed with his favorite cologne. He's not groping or taking the hug too far. It's just right.

"Thank you." He whispers. Then I step back.

We stand lost in time until I hear a throat clear behind me. I glance back and remember we're not alone.

"Darius, I think you know everyone." I sweep through the ladies, and they shake hands. "We thought we'd invite you out for drinks to get reacquainted and see if there's a way we can help you and Delicious Chocolates."

He adjusts into a wide-leg stand, crossing his arms over his chest. "Drinks with all of you?"

"Yes." I clear my throat, looking off for a moment. "I heard you mention expending opportunities to businesses in the area and we have a business."

"Congratulations! What do you guys do?" He smiles.

"We have an elite concierge service."

"What exactly does that mean?" He steps closer.

"That's why I'm inviting you to have drinks with us." His eyes sweep my face, and if I were a few shades darker, he'd see me blush. "Stop acting like you don't want to."

"All right Charlee, I'll bite?"

"Oh really…" slipped out and a smoldering hue fills his eyes, and an irresistibly devastating grin spreads across his face.

He takes another step, and I have to tilt my head to maintain eye contact. "Only if you want me to." I inhale, filling my lungs with his scent. His voice is so low I would have missed it if my eyes didn't drop to his mouth.

"So, tell me, Charlee Raine, I meet with you and your posse for drinks. Then what?"

"My posse?"

"Yeah, y'all strolled across the lawn looking like Charlie's Angels."

"Oh, you're a sly one. Long as you don't call me Charlie Brown again." I joke trying to lower that damn heat rising in my body.

"Nah, I learned my lesson with that one."

Is that a coy look? Jesus, I'm in trouble.

"Get a room." I hear someone hiss behind me. I stick out my tongue, and they laugh.

"My angels are getting restless. So, meet us at Smith & Jameson. Tomorrow at seven. And hurry, you know your mother hates waiting." I pat his shoulder and turn to walk away.

"Why do people who always run late hate waiting?" He asks with an eyebrow piqued.

"Why on earth would I have the answer to that Mr. Grant?"

"Oh, we all know the answer to that question," Taylor says, and the guys laugh as they turn towards their cars leaving us alone.

"I'll be there under one condition," Darius says.

I stop. "And that is?"

He pulls out a cellphone and clicks around. Then he passes it to me. "Add your number."

I hold the phone, training my facial muscles not to out me. I feel the pressure mounting in my chest again.

It's just a number. Ten to be exact. I look up and see his waiting face, not missing the twitch in his jaw. He's nervous too.

I adjust my purse strap and pass him my bible. I enter my number and hit the bright green icon on the screen. I hear my phone vibrate and disconnect the call.

I flick the phone back into his hands, taking back my bible.

"I'll see you tomorrow. Enjoy brunch with your mother." I turn to catch up with the guys.

"How do you know about brunch?" He walks beside me, and I slow my pace.

"Miss Janice is not missing an opportunity to show off that killer dress." I laugh. I slow the pace as I see the guys ahead. "It's good seeing you."

"Same to you. So, why didn't you return any of my calls?"

I stop and turn around. "You wanted a new life. The best way to do that is with a clean slate. It made the transition less complicated."

He nods, I don't miss the tense squint of his eyes. "We were never a complication."

"That's debatable." I take a deep breath. "It's best not to go there."

"That your whip." His head tilts towards my ride.

"Yeah." I smile.

"Daddy still spoiling his princess." His words cut.

"This is the complication I'm talking about." I cut back. "Look I gotta go."

"Right. I'll see you tomorrow." He looks past me. "You ladies enjoy your Resurrection Sunday. Charlee I hope you have a day as beautiful as you are." His eyes caress my face. "And you are wearing that dress." He kisses my cheek, turns, and walks away.

I watch him walk away, and I want to pull out my phone. The swagger in his walk, the confidence in his stride.

"Darius is on a mission." Taylor is beside me.

"You noticed?" I can't pull my eyes away until he rounds the side of the church.

"If his chocolates tempting as he is, this contract will be worth the trouble." Hunter rubs her belly.

My cheek is tingling from his touch, and I'm torn. So many emotions are flooding my mind and my body. I'm elated, shocked, horny, confused. *Torn.*

"I kind of feel like I walked into a trap."

"You should," Harper says, looping her arm through mine. "He didn't seem too surprised by our invitation."

Hunter glances back down the sidewalk. "He always had a soft spot for you Charlee. Maybe you should let this one go. You could find another business."

"Nah," I dig deep for my sassy self, "I got this in the bag. Look I gotta run." I turn and kiss each of their cheeks. We say our goodbyes. Minutes later I'm back in my car. I replay the morning from running late to watching Darius walk away.

Our relationship is complicated, but it's also one that makes it easy to talk with him. I doubt signing him will take more than a casual meeting over drinks, them something more detailed. So, I'm guessing three meetings tops.

I can handle three meetings. But can I handle Darius? I doubt that is humanly possible. The possibility increases if I keep my panties on and my heart free of him.

What else will make this possible? I pull into my gate bringing my car to a stop.

I can schedule meetings at S&J. Controlling my environment and the meeting times will help keep my anxiety to a minimum. This will also limit my exposure to him.

Less time alone gives me hope that I can fight off my natural pull towards him. Plus, he travels a lot, which means he's in town now, but knowing him, he'll jet off to another country tomorrow.

Maybe this won't be so bad after all. I get out of the car liking the thought of this more.

Austin is a decent size town. We can dwell in the same city without me going loco again. I close the door behind me. I walk inside my townhouse dropping my purse and keys on the island in my kitchen.

That settles it. I'm doing it.

I'm signing Delicious Chocolates.

CHAPTER 4

DARIUS

The line outside Smith & Jameson intrigues me. I took a chance and sent Charlee a text message asking her to meet me for lunch. She accepted.

I'm sitting outside waiting for her car to arrive because Charlee is always late. And I need the time to make a few calls.

Today has been a disaster. Real estate in Austin is worse than I thought. The agent is hopeful. I'm not.

My entire team is temporarily set up in San Francisco. This move will cost me a fortune, and my VP is not yet on board. I have a small window to make it happen.

I see Charlee's car speed around a corner in my direction. I shake my head laughing. She needs to set her clocks fast or something because she's going to hurt someone driving like a mad woman. I get out of my rental making it to her car as she cuts the engine.

I open her door, and her smile melts away the tension I'm feeling.

"Hey you," she says.

"Hey yourself. Can I help you with something?"

"Hold my bag for a second." She passes her purse, fiddling around in her car. "Okay, I'm ready." She reclaims the bag standing beside me. "It didn't go well."

"Not at all. Should we go somewhere else?" I motion to the line now wrapping the building.

"I got this. You're rolling with me."

"Oh, my bad." I tease. "Lead the way."

Charlee walks pass the line through the door. She stops in front of the hostess and exchanging air kisses. I take in the relaxed environment. There's 90s R&B playing. The volume is low enough to hear the hum of the people talking. This place is new to me. I glance back at Charlee working her magic. I hear part of their conversation when she asks whether the VIP room is available.

"Mind if we eat in a conference room?" She asks me.

"I'm low-key as long as the food is good."

"The food is phenomenal," Charlee says, then turns back to the hostess. "Set us up in the conference room. Right, this way Darius." She motions inside, and I follow. "Smith & Jameson is family owned and operated. The owners are good people and clients of Platinum Prestige."

"Don't we need menus," I ask.

"No, sir. The food is provided by food trucks. It's back this way. So, tell me about today."

We walk and talk. I tell her about running around all day. "The issue is the lack of viable options for build a full factory and an office," I say opening a door for her.

"I might be able to help with that. First food." She turns with a flourish. "Pick your poison."

The courtyard is filled with large food trucks. I see barbecue, Thai, Ethiopian, even Southern Cuisine.

"And there are more around the corner." She says.

"I already know what I'm getting."

"Boy gets your barbecue, and I'll meet you back here in fifteen minutes."

"You got it!"

We split, and I already feel better. I watch her walk away, loving the fit of her jeans.

Food first, Charlee second.

The aroma is indescribable. I order all of my favorites, sure I've died and gone to barbecue heaven. I buy ribs, sausage, brisket, and a mound of potato salad. My tray weighs a good ten pounds.

I see Charlee ahead.

"You do know this is a lunch break?"

"Stop sassing and get me to a table."

"Bossy…bossy."

I walk a few steps behind to get a good look at the sexy sway in her hips. She's cracking jokes, and I'm basking in the ease of *us*. She talks, I listen. I flirt a little, and she flirts back.

We fall back into our old pattern. And the conversation doesn't stop until we reach the conference room. She selects a chair, and I spread out my food in front of the next seat over.

We sit.

"I'll pray." Charlee reaches for my hand, bowing her head.

I know it's against good form, but I watch her, holding her hand a little tighter. This is the Charlee, most people miss. She's crazy and wild. But it's the soft parts of her that she reserves for very few people are what make her so unique. And it's a quality I've always appreciated.

Well, maybe not enough, if my mother's assessment is right. *Did Charlee really want me to stay?* I'll table that thought for another time.

"Amen." She reaches for her fork.

"I missed you," I say.

"You should."

"Sassy-ass Charlee." My head falls back, and I laugh.

We eat in silence for a while. My mind travels down memory lane until I'm back at our college graduation. She had no plans, and I wanted to start my own business. I thought she'd want to join me, but she didn't. Now I'm back with the only woman I've ever loved, trying to figure out how to get a second chance. Sure, I've had women since our relationship ended. But I'm back where I belong.

Charlee props her elbows on the table, "Let me hear it."

"Hear what?" I'm sure I have barbecue sauce everywhere, but this food is that good.

"What's going on with this search? I can't take your long face, and I don't have all day." She folds her hands.

I clean my hands and sit back. "I thought this morning would have produced more options than it did. We went from Round Rock to San Marcos. The prices on real estate are insane."

"Yeah. Austin is booming right now. What are you looking for?"

I give her an intense look. I don't know *this* Charlee.

"What?" She squeals.

"I'm shocked I guess."

She flicks a dismissive hand. "I know a few people. I told you we have a business. So, now, I move in a different circle."

"Boss lady." I tease.

"Stop. Tell me what you need, specifically." She pulls out her phone, and I'm legit shocked. And then I remember she's the woman who kindly planted a ball in my face. And I chuckle leaning forward.

"What's so funny?"

"I was thinking about how you planted that ball in my face for calling you Charlie Brown."

Charlee laughs, holding her stomach. "Oh, you should have seen your face and all the blood."

"I thought you were psycho."

"I was. I hated people calling me Charlie Brown. And I had a crush on you. So, it made the ribbing worse."

"Crush? Wait, why is this the first time I'm hearing about this crush?"

"Because your head would have swelled to the size of a hot air balloon. That's why you didn't know about the crush."

"I was a good kid."

"No, your mamma thought you were a good kid. I knew differently." She said with enough sass to make me kiss her right now.

"And what did you know Charlee Raine?"

"That all the girls wanted you. Even then." Her eyes linger on my mouth.

"And what about now?" I moisten my bottom lip ready to accept the invitation I see in her eyes. "Because I'm only concerned about one girl."

"And who's that?" She turns in the seat. I get a good view of her full breast and the memories of old times feel like yesterday. Because Charlee brings all that sass to the bed, and just the thought has my johnson tuned into this exchange.

"Oh, you don't know?" I take a chance and run a finger along her soft cheek.

"Can't say I run with any girls, I run with grown-ass women."

"Well, pardon me, Miss Grown-Ass Woman."

She spins in the chair, and now her knees are between my legs, and we're facing each other.

"Cut the shit." She demands. This woman is like air to my lungs. *How did I forget?*

I shrug. "I came back for you."

"Bull shit." She tries to push back, and I grab the back of her knees pulling her closer. Her eyes burn with desire, and I'm all in.

"Have I ever minced my words?"

"No."

"Then why don't you believe me?"

"Because you left." She whispers.

"Because you said go."

"And you left." She pushes back.

"We've always spoken plain. I asked you to come with me."

"As an afterthought. Plus what was I supposed to do, leave my mother? No, you had your mind made up, and I wasn't part of the equation." She crosses her arms over her chest.

"You must be mistaken."

She pops to her feet. "It's over now." She tosses the dirty dishes on the empty trays. She turns to leave the room, but I beat her to the door.

"Like hell it is."

"Don't do this." Her eyes won't meet mine. "We had a great lunch. I'll make a few calls about your building." She turns and gives me a fake smile. But it's the unshed tears in her eyes that cut me.

"I call bull shit."

"Call all you want Darius."

"Talk to me Charlee. What did you want me to do? Stay here and work some dead-end job. Then what? You'd regret being tied to your broke boyfriend."

"Don't you dare do that. I *never* cared about your money." She poked a finger in my chest.

"You didn't have to. Your father. Your family. You're friends. All rich ass, stuck up, looking down their noses at the poor little bused kid from the East side."

We're yelling, and I'm thankful we're off in a back room. This conversation is needed to move forward.

"Charlee, I couldn't stay here *and* have you. I couldn't look at you and be a man. I had to leave and find my way. What kind of man would I be if I sat around waiting for your father to offer me a job? Or I can't afford to give you the life you're accustomed to?"

"You'd look like the kind of man who stays."

"No, I'd look like a fuckin' leech." Her head jerks back.

"Don't play your fuckin' head games with me, Darius. You had me, you lost me. Now step aside." The fire in her eyes could set this building ablaze.

"I got some *shit* for yo ass." I dip my head until my lips are a breath from hers. "I'm back. So if you got a dude, drop him. Ain't nobody and nothing better than us."

"Cocky ain't we."

"Than a muthafucka'."

She takes a step closer, her chest brushes mine, and my hands ache to touch her.

"And what makes you so sure, I want your *broke-ass* back."

"Baby, keep playing with me and you'll see you ain't the only grown-ass in the building. Do it, Charlee Raine." I move aside.

"Fuck you, Darius." She heads out of the room.

"Oh I plan to, and I'll have you calling me *zaddy*. Mark my words."

CHAPTER 5

CHARLEE

I'm pissed. I want to call an emergency meeting with the guys, but I'd have to tell them I ran from him.

I sit in my car, nibbling on the inside of my cheek. And I could call my mother, but she's president of the Darius Grant club.

"I still love Darius."

I hear the words, and it hurts. But I refuse to lie to myself. I wish it weren't true, that I could take back my love and my heart back. But he's right. That moment in junior high sealed the deal.

We remained inseparable until the week after we graduated from college. He'd been beside me as I went from a girl to a woman. He was my first real kiss, he was my first lover. I thought he'd be my husband and the father of my children. But his ambition changed it all.

But what is love? *Really?*

"A fuckin' fraud." I let out a gruff sigh.

Why me? Why did he have to come back? I was living my best life...*sort of*. I have everything and nothing. I party and travel and date but inside I feel hollow.

I came back for you.

His words sink deeper into my soul and are seated shotgun with my heartbreak. Every man that I loved and trusted left me. First my father, then Darius. And I refuse to let him back, only to leave again.

I turn on my car. I can't sit here thinking about him or my father. I have to boss up, that means sticking to business. I can connect him with some leads, get his company on board with Platinum Prestige, and then I can maybe reward myself with a little getaway.

I smile. I like the sound of that. I can think of only one person that will see the silver lining in this whole ordeal and who will help me get past my feelings. I speed dial, Harper.

"I'm flying to you."

"What will it be sweet tea or wine?"

"Tequila." My voice cracks. I grip the steering wheel barely holding it together the moment I hear her voice.

"Oh, brother." I hear her moving around on the other end.

Harper is the mother hen of the group. It's weird knowing Hunter is the first one of us to become a mother. First to Ben's daughter Zoe and now to the twins, she's carrying. I always thought it would've been Harper.

"I'll be ready. I have tequila, popcorn, and I think I have a bar of chocolate."

"No chocolate, *pleeeeease* no chocolate." Why am I so emotional? I felt the tears welling up earlier, and now they're back too.

"Sweetie, we'll get through this. Promise." I nod. She can't see me, but I believe her.

"And ice cream, lots and lots of ice cream."

"Of course."

"And this is why I love you." We share a laugh. "I'm almost there."

I disconnect the call. My squad is ten women strong. We're all friends, but naturally, we fall in clusters. My cluster consists of Harper, Hunter, and Taylor.

I drive through town slowly making my way to her place. She recently started working for fine-ass Liam Walsh, and I laughed at Harper's flight from him the first week or so of their acquaintance. Now I understand how a man can turn you on and drive you insane in the same breath.

Because Darius does that to me. The fact that we can fall back in sync after so long doesn't surprise me. My body is still humming from his touch, and the fact that I haven't had a real lover since him makes my plight ten times worse.

I park, and the moment I step on the porch her door opens.

"*Heifa* you would have that shit on a silver platter."

"Nothing but the best." She smiles, but I read the

concern in her eyes. She opens an arm to me, and I accept her hug. "Come, inside."

I kick off my shoes and drop to her couch much like she dropped to mine a few weeks ago. I stare at the ceiling.

"How'd it go?" Harper asks.

"It was good, then it was great, then it was awful. Yeah, really awful." I look over at her on the low seat.

"How much time are we talking about?"

"Two hours tops."

"Sheesh." She pulls her legs beneath her, leaning into the arm of the couch.

"Pretty much," I tell her about everything from the moment I pulled up. By the time I get to the moment where I stomped out, I'm livid again. "And guess what he said?"

"Before or after you said fuck you?" Her eyes twinkle with humor.

"You know what," I sit up, "I don't need your sass, I have enough drama in my life right now."

"Yes, ma'am. But what did he say Charlee." Then she makes the motion of locking her mouth.

"I don't believe you for one second." I toss a pillow at her, and she blocks. "He said, I'll have you calling me zaddy."

"Daaayyyyuuuummmmm." She gave her best *Friday* impression, and I die laughing.

"God, I promise this shit ain't funny."

"Good, because I seem to recall a certain someone

running for snacks when Liam and I had our showdown."

"That's putting it mildly." I smile. "I'm known for a good f-bomb. You, it's like an eclipse or something."

Harper laughs. "So, how much of this is about Darius and how much is about your father?"

"Way to go right in Harp." I look away.

"I gotta wear my Charlee shoes on this one. You've been tap dancing around these issues for years."

"Years?" I sit up, and she takes the cushion beside me. I'm experiencing a gamut of difficult emotions. The overarching one is grief. It's shoved down deep and seeing Darius brings it back to the surface. "I guess both. I just can't trust either of them. Not like I used to."

"Why?" I drop my head to her shoulder, and we fall back.

"Is that new?" There's a beautiful crystal butterfly on the shelf in front of us.

"Yes. It's a gift from Liam."

"How's that going?" I prop my feet on the coffee table.

"No diverting." She insists.

"I just need a moment."

She nods. "It's going. We're working well together. I've just never had a man like him in my life."

"Like what?"

"I don't know," she fidgets with her flowy dress. "He takes up so much space."

"I've never heard that one before." I chuckle as I examine the pattern on the fabric in her hands.

"There's no other way to describe it. He's physically big. But it's like he's occupying my thoughts, my heart, my dreams. I can't seem to shake him."

"Do you love him?"

"That's impossible. Right?"

"Nothing is impossible sweetheart." They've only been seeing each other for a month. But Liam proposed and she accepted. "I've seen the way he looks at you. And I don't doubt his love for a second...or yours."

"Mine?" Her breath catches.

It's my turn to nod. "That man proposed to you in the middle of Target. And look at that rock."

She wiggles her fingers. "It's all scary. The moment I decide to throw in the towel. Here he comes."

"It's the damndest thing." I squeeze her arm a little tighter.

"Charlee, the same look you see in Liam's eyes is matched by the love in Darius' eyes yesterday." I try to pull away. "Don't you dare. You're always dishing out your tough love. It's time to woman up and take this ribbing."

"Well damn."

"You can't keep punishing him for what your father did. That man has loved you since junior high. His world was all about you and your world was all about him."

"Then he ruined it." The thought rips through my insides.

"I don't see it like that."

"Okay Polly Anna, how do you see it?"

"Imma get you for that one." She bumps me with her shoulder. "We are complicated women. Most men can't handle our lives, our wealth, our families. It takes a certain kind of man to go toe-to-toe with you Charlee. And I think that man is Darius."

I let her words sink in, and I open my mouth to refute them. But she continues, "And I seem to recall a wise heifa say…"

"Oh, you are trying me tonight!"

Harper laughs, "You said, that maybe Liam just caught me off guard. Couldn't the same be true of you? You're one of the toughest women I know. Sure, you've had some knocks, we all have. But for a woman who is always speed dating, always championing us finding a boo, why would you run from the one man you've always loved?"

"Because I'm a chicken shit when it comes to him. What will I do when he picks up and leaves again?"

"Hell, go with him."

"Liam has got you feeling yourself. That means the *d* must be good."

Her head falls back, and our laughter fills the air. But she didn't deny it.

"We're not the same women we were in college Charlee. If it goes south, we'll do like we always do."

"Kick ass and take names," I yell.

"That's the Charlee I know and love."

We sit up. I have to face off with Darius, and I'm feeling more like myself.

"Thank you, Harper."

"Anytime love."

"Things must be going well for you guys."

"Most days. Others, I fight with the same lingering doubts. Yours is that he'll leave again, mine is that he'll turn back into a frog. Adulting is hard."

I stand and pull Harper to her feet. "I think we could take this challenge like we're taking on the business."

"And how's that?"

"Do it scared." I declare.

"I'm down with that. Now, get going because I refuse to be late with you."

"Well, go on with your shady ass. Besides I'm never late, I just love making a grand entrance."

"Lies! It's a surprise you still have rubber on your tires. Get going! Beat him there. Show him you're not the same Charlee Raine."

I head towards the door.

"One last thing…"

"Yes, oh wise one." I tease.

"You already love him. The least you can do is see if it can work. If not, we go back to speed dating. But, what if it does? What if this time we both get our men?"

"Oh hell, now I know it's time to go. You're back to that Disney shit."

I laugh all the way to the car. I feel better. I can't say I'm fully onboard with what Darius has in mind—or Harper. But I'm open. Even if it's to get a little *d* for myself.

CHAPTER 6

I drove around in circles after lunch with Charlee. I told my truth, but my delivery overshadowed the words I've practiced for months. I enter the wooden door of S&J, and I'm surprised by seeing Charlee over the shoulder of the hostess.

She's at the bar talking. I stop to drink her in. I can tell by the sway of her hands and the animation of her face that she's telling a joke. Then the men huddled around her laugh.

I'm grateful our mothers are friends. I was able to beg my mother for a little information. I know Charlee's not seeing anyone seriously or I'd be in a jealous rage.

But infidelity was never our issue. My hangups about what I bring to the relationship separated us for too long. The success of Delicious Chocolates made me a millionaire, and I'm not stopping. The next stop is the billionaire's club.

I can't let my old hangups ruin this moment. I was the poor kid trying to hang with the rich kids. I excelled academically and earned a scholarship to the best private school in Austin. That's how and when I met Charlee and her friends. She never made me feel different, but she didn't have to.

I *was* different.

I still am.

Except now, I carry my difference as a distinguishing characteristic instead of a burden. Because for all of her acceptance, Charlee will never fully get how it felt to be me around her, for me to be me in her world.

I stroll up to the bar tired of seeing the crowd gathered around my woman.

I dip in kissing her lips. "Charlee Raine."

"Staking your claim I see."

"I told you why I'm here, and I mean it." I pull back taking the seat over her shoulder. I'm close enough to smell the soft, sweet scent of her perfume.

"Darius, I'd like to introduce you to Asher Smith and Dylan Jameson."

I shake their hands.

"It's a pleasure," I say, then it dawns on me. "Of Smith & Jameson?"

There's a collective nod.

"We have a few minutes before the guys show up. But I thought it would help to have a chat with Asher and Dylan. I told them about your issues with locating a building. I think they can help." Charlee says.

"I'd like that." I stand, and I reach for her hand.

"I'll be here when you return." She smiles, her eyes dart to mine then back toward Asher and Dylan.

"Can you give us a moment alone?" I ask.

"Yeah, let's meet in the conference room in 15 minutes." Asher points over his shoulder.

"That works. I'll see you then." They walk off in the direction of the VIP room, and I turn to Charlee. "We need to talk."

I spin her around on the barstool, turning her body to me.

"How are you?" The corners of her eyes soften, but I know I'm not out of the woods.

"I've been better."

"You look beautiful tonight." I reach for a curl draped over her shoulder, wrapping it around my finger. She's wearing an off the shoulder blouse with jeans and heels. I glance away for a moment. Not wanting her to read my lust-filled thoughts.

"Thank you." She leans closer fiddling with the front of my shirt. And I turn back to her.

The music and soft chatter fill the air, but the people disappear the moment our eyes lock. She lowers her feet to the floor bringing us face to face.

"So tell me, what am I up against?"

"What do you mean Mr. Grant?" She pulls a glossy lip between her teeth.

"I told you why I'm back. How hard of a fight are we talking about?"

"Depends on how well you perform tonight."

"Oh, it's like that?"

A slow sexy smile crosses her face. And I yearn to have her alone, to touch her, to taste her. The heat in her eyes draws me closer without moving an inch.

"Maybe...."

I capture the word in my mouth. Her lips are warm and sweet. Our tongues mate, getting reacquainted. She moans and its the green light I need to dive deeper holding nothing back. I wrap my hands around her waist bringing her body closer to mine. The fire I remember pulses through my veins. This seals her fate because there's no way I'm not having her tonight. I reluctantly pull back. Her sweet tongue darts out for one last sample.

God, I missed her. I send up a quick prayer, *Please don't let me mess this up again.*

Charlee reaches for a napkin and gently rubs it against my mouth. No doubt to remove her gloss from my face. I kiss her again greedy for more. This time she sits back.

"Your place or mine?"

"Yours." The fire in her eyes is not of anger but of red hot passion.

"Are you going to give us a shot? I want you Charlee, and I plan to have all of you tonight. But I ain't on no one night stand bull."

I bring my lips to hers unable to stop kissing her. Her moan is my air.

"Say the words, Charlee Raine," I demand then I'm

making out with this woman again, in public and I don't give a damn. I've waited for years, and she's as tempting as ever.

"We can try again. But if you break my heart again…." The words trail off, and I feel the shake of her body against mine.

"Nah baby, this shit here is it." I lift her chin bringing her eyes to mine. "I mean it Charlee." Her smile chases away the doubt I see staring back at me.

I'll show her.

"I have a meeting." I remind her, as she wipes at my mouth again. "And so we're clear, we are *us*."

Her head bobs and her eyes fill with tears.

"Baby, don't cry. We got this." I cup her face in my hands, kissing her soft and slow.

"Now get before people think I'm a wuss." She smoothes out the wrinkles in my shirt, her eyes not meeting mine.

"Charlee, look at me, baby." Her dark eyes settle on mine. "I won't fuck this up."

"I'll hold you to that."

I kiss her one last time. Then I stand to head back to the conference room.

"I'll be back."

"I'll be here."

I retrace the steps I took earlier. This time with Charlee on my side. I glance back, and she's watching me. I toss a cocky wink, and I hear her laughter. I'll die trying to keep a smile on her face because I meant what I said. She's mine now, and now it's time for me to secure our future.

I hear the chime of my ringer. I pull it out of my pocket, it's my Vice President, Shyann. "What's up?"

"We need you back pronto."

"I'm heading into a meeting, can it wait?" I stand outside the conference room.

"No. Jack the weasel is trying to raise the prices again. We have a large custom order due in Europe. You know shipping alone takes time. This is with corporate keepsakes due on Friday."

"I'll be there tomorrow. Can you hold it afloat until then?"

"I got you. I won't let it sink." She chuckles.

"All right. See you then." I disconnect taking a deep breath.

My operation is booming but small. Part of my desire to move here is to build a custom facility. I need to hire more employees. Then we'll train them on my proprietary method of creating corporate chocolate products.

For now, we all wear a hundred hats. We all roll up our sleeves to make, package, and ship chocolate. No task is too big or too small. But I know if Shyann called it must be severe.

I make a quick call to prep for a flight tonight. Then I head into the conference room. Looks like I'm taking my Charlee on a little adventure.

CHAPTER 7

CHARLEE

e are us. I inhale three shots the moment I see Darius disappear around the corner. That was our saying. The way we said it's us against the world.

What did I just do? What did I just do? What did I just do?

The burning sensation of the tequila takes off the edge. I drop my head to my forearm resting on the bar. I take a deep breath through my nose and out my mouth. I should be shooting flames after those damn shots.

I glance up when I feel someone sit next to me.

"There's got to be a rule against pregnant women sitting at the bar." I sit up and rub Hunter's stomach. She *was* the sassiest, globetrotting friend I had and now, she's different, in the best possible way. "Hey babies," I whisper to her growing bump. "Let's find a table before your husband have both of our asses."

"Not until you talk to me." I see the determined look on her face.

"What did I do now?"

"I don't know. You tell me."

"What's up with the riddles Hunt?"

"I know something's going on. You're throwing back shots like they're Skittles, and Harper is watching you in her true mother hen mode." She flicks her head towards the side wall. There are the guys. "I can only deduct that it's Darius. So, are you going to tell me or do I have to find him and ask for myself?"

"There's really nothing to tell." I shrug.

I honestly don't know where to start. I've accepted that I will try this relationship with Darius again. Which I can't believe. But my heart is racing from the tequila and fear. Yet, my ego won't let me run. I guess I'll be popping Skittles until….until whenever.

"Fine. Have it your way?" Hunter pops up from the barstool, with my help, and stalks towards the conference room.

"Where are you waddling to?" I suck at holding back my laugh.

"Don't you dare laugh at me." She calls over her shoulder. "I'm going to talk with Darius."

"Oh no, you don't." I block her from entering the back suites. "Let me explain."

"Do it fast. My feet are swollen, my back hurts, and I'm hungry." Her arms cross resting over her babies.

"I'll be glad when you have these babies. I'm tired of you bossing me around."

"Girl, please. If it's good for the goose."

I cock my head to the side. "*Heifa*, did you just call me a goose?"

"Spill it Charlee."

"See, you better be glad I'm fighting with Harper to be the godmother to my babies, or I'd let your ass have it." I joke, but her eyes are playing Jedi mind tricks. "I really hate you guys. Fine! I plan to sleep with Darius tonight."

Hunter gasps.

"I know. I know. I realize I still love him. Which sucks because I'm barely surviving as it is. And then he said he came back for me. I 'bout dropped a brick. Like what the hell! My vajayjay is like yay...and my heart is like hell naw. I mean have you seen the man. And I'm like might as well jump in with two feet. You know what I'm saying?" The words flow like a mighty river. It's one massive, disrespectful run-on mess. "I need another Skittle."

I execute an about-face and head back to the bar.

"Oh no, you don't. It's time for an emergency meeting." She flicks her hand towards the door and the guys

"We'll lose our table," I whine.

"Ain't nobody worried about that damn table."

Hunter drags me through S&J like I'm her child and I let her. Not because I'm tipsy but because I'm a wreck. My potty mouth has gone from spicy to vulgar. What scares me the most is I thought I was over him? It's been nearly six years, and I'm still an absolute mess when it comes to this man.

When did I become this woman?

The delegation is waiting outside the doors. We huddle on the sidewalk much like yesterday. This is my life after 24-hours of Darius. I groan.

"I vote to forget Delicious Chocolates." We barely clear the doorway, and she's already conducting the meeting.

Half the guys are confused because they didn't attend church yesterday. Taylor quickly brings them up to speed.

"Charlee's ex Darius Grant is the owner of Delicious Chocolates. He made an announcement about partnering with local businesses. Then he staked a claim on Charlee."

"Quite ad-libbing and stick to the facts," I demand.

"That is a fact." Taylor counters and I try to ignore the show of support from the others.

"Finish the damn recap." I huff.

Taylor finishes and the seven of them are looking at me. Harper is at my side, and Hunter is on the other. I see the concern in their eyes. But I have to let this shit go. Either I'm going to trust him or not. Because I refuse to walk around in this constant state of arousal and fear.

"I'm good. Really." I elbow Harper. "He caught me by surprise I admit, and there's history there."

"Do you still love him?" Taylor asks.

"Yes. But I'm fighting a lost cause because it feels like I've always loved him. That no other guy worked because he wasn't Darius. So, I figure. Give it a grown-ass woman sort of effort."

"Then what?" Parker asks.

"Then either we'll have another wedding to plan, or I move on." I try to shrug it off, but if it took me six years to get here, it could take me a lifetime to scrub him from my mind for good.

"How does your mother feel about it?" Jordan asks.

"She's the president of the Darius Grant fan club." They laugh. "Honestly, this is the second time I'm admitting it to myself. I'll talk to her later. Right now I'm winging it."

"Then why agree to sleep with him?" Hunter asks.

I glance over at her. I envision his smile and my stomach flutters. "To take the edge off."

"Won't that make it harder to decide?" Taylor asks.

"Probably. But I've told him, yes and now I'm gonna jump. It's what I've wanted, and I refuse to run scared."

"What if he leaves again?" Taylor counters.

"Then the ass kicking will commence," Harper says. We all burst into laughter. I fold over about to die. "What?! Somebody had to say it."

We laugh until we cry and when I stand up fully my guys pull closer.

"Charlee, you say I'm tough, but you're tougher. I say fight for your man. I think he's worth it." Hunter wraps an arm around my waist.

"And if I bring up the average, your spunk gives us life. So, he will have to deal with all of us if this situation goes south." Harper loops her arm through mine. "I say get your man too."

The other ladies chime in, one by one, giving me the support I need to follow my heart.

"Charlee if you're going to do this. I think you should plan to meet with your dad." Taylor is the last to speak. My chest burns from holding my breath. "I think speaking to your dad will give you and Darius a real shot."

I release Hunter and Harper. I step forward and hug Taylor tight. She's our processor, but unlike a computer, she's all heart. She knows the struggles I have with my father. We both are honorary members of the deadbeat dad's club.

"Promise me?" She whispers in my ear.

"I will."

Taylor pulls back. "Then you have my blessing too."

"I'm the luckiest woman alive. I love you guys."

"We love you too!" They sing.

"Now let's eat because I'm starving," Hunter says.

We laugh our way towards S&J when I see Darius waiting outside the door. The ladies tease and give him finger waves as they enter, leaving us alone.

"You good?" He asks pulling my body against his. I feel the firmness beneath the suit, and my mind travels to later tonight.

"I'm better than good. How'd the meeting go?"

"It was informative but short. I got a call from my office. I need to head out."

"Already?" I feel my hope drop with my heart. I stand up, stepping back wrapping my arms around myself.

"Yes, It can't be helped."

"Okay. Well, travel safely. And call me when you get back." *It begins...* I open the door.

"Woah...wait a minute, not so fast." He closes the door. "I want you to come with me."

"Come with you?" That surprises me.

"Yes, Charlee. I told you, I'm serious. The best way I can show you...is to show you." He kisses me and peers down into my eyes. "So, how about a trip to San Francisco?"

"When?"

"Now woman." His cocky-ass smile is killing me softly. He slips his hands around my waist, bringing me back to him.

"But I need to pack."

"All I need is you. I'll take care of the rest."

"What?!" I cock my head to the side. "You got it like that now?" And the ease of having fun with him returns.

"Say yes Charlee Raine…." Darius nibbles on my neck.

My head falls back and right before his mouth takes mine I whisper, "Yes."

CHAPTER 8

"*A*re you a member?"

I glance over at his profile. Then Darius gives me a devilish smile.

"A member of what? What did I miss?" He laughs putting his computer aside. We've been in the air less than thirty minutes after I literally grabbed an overnight bag from my house.

I study his lean brown face, his beard, his goatee as I wonder what the hell this man is talking about now. I shake my head taking a moment to appreciate his fineness.

He was always handsome, but in a suit and tie, flying high in his private plane, it's all a total turn on. Wait *flying high*…my heart rate kicks up a notch.

"The mile high club?"

He nods. "Are you Charlee Raine?"

"No." The temperature increases and I feel a silly grin across my face the moment he crosses the aisle.

"Good. It looks like we're about to cross another first off our list." He moves my laptop to the vacant seat, my phone and headphones go next.

His eyes graze my body from my eyes to my shoulders to my breast. He licks his lips and travels south settling at the source of my furnace. I clench my thighs tight, no doubt my panties are soaked. And the twinkle in his eyes tells me he knows it.

"You're such a tease," I tell him.

"Come with me, baby."

I take his hand, and he leads me to a bedroom. "Who has a bedroom on a plane?"

"I need it for long flights. Lift your arms." He removes my shirt as if this is a regular occurrence, brushing his finger over the lace trimming my bra. He kisses the exposed flesh, then lowers to my feet. My shoes, pants, and panties join my shirt on the floor. "One item left."

My knees are weak as he circles my body. He unhooks my bra and catches the weight of my breasts before they fall. He gently squeezes and pulls on my nipples, feathering kisses across my shoulder, up to my neck and latching on to my earlobe.

"I hope I don't embarrass you." The heat of his breath against my ear is driving me insane. My nipples are hard thanks to his playing, and I'm ready to play too. I throw my ass back against his thickness.

"You're gonna have me screaming like a lunatic." I laugh.

"That's the plan." His voice is like silk. Then his hand finds the dampness between my thighs and a finger slips inside.

I gasp reaching for anything that will keep me on my feet because this man ain't playing. He's applying pressure to my pearl, stroking, filling my ear with all the ways he plans to love me.

My head falls back to his shoulder, my mouth searching for his. I'm about to rain all over his hand, and he's still in a damn suit.

"This shit ain't right."

"It's better than right, this is perfection." He brands me, biting on my neck as I see the end drawing near. My world consists of him, and the mounting pressure as his hand works overtime.

The door slams closed. *Zip.* Rip of plastic.

"Hands on the wall." He commands.

His hand is suddenly gone, and I groan in agony until he enters me. His dick filling me from wall to wall, stretching and molding my core to accommodate his thickness.

"Fuck!"

I don't know if it's him or me. But his long strokes have me screaming. Then he spins me to the bed, and I'm facing down. My ass is in the air, he's gripping my hips making his presence known.

"Darius." My kitty kat is singing his praises as my walls contract.

"Let me hear it." His ass is still cocky.

I shake my head. I refuse. But the shit feels so good. I throw my ass back.

"Fuck!" That was him.

Two can play this game. Then he increases the tempo. Skin smacking again skin, our panting fills the air. He smacks my ass, and the sensation travels up my spine.

"I'm about to…." Darius pulls out. "Imma kill you."

"Say it, Charlee Raine." He kisses the left cheek.

"I hate your ass."

"I love your fat ass." He kisses the right cheek. "Maybe you need some motivation."

He spreads a hand over my lower back and drives so deep I'm screaming *zaddy*, and we're coming at the same time. The force of it overwhelms me, and I'm dead on my feet. The moment I think I'm about to face plant into the bed Darius pulls me into his arms.

He lowers me to the bed. My eyes dip close.

"You did all that with your damn clothes on?"

"I ain't done with you yet."

He removes his shirt exposing his chiseled chest and perfect abs. His pants drop to the floor, and his body is perfect. I catch a second wind, and my lady parts are thankful we said yes.

"Ready baby?" He climbs in the bed.

"Damn right!"

Darius covers himself for the second time and enters me, then wraps my legs around his waist.

The first round was to prove a point and give us both a release. This time, he loves me until we're both breathless.

He immediately falls asleep. But I can't sleep. I roll over on my side and think about the past two days. This is unreal. I kiss his chest.

His moan makes me smile. Then his eyes open.

"I love you Charlee." His finger runs down the bridge of my nose. "I can't remember a time I haven't loved you. Do you believe that?"

I see the heart-stopping tenderness in his gaze. Loving him might be the death of me.

"Yes." I'm caught up in my emotions. He's overwhelming in a soul-soothing type of way. It feels new and old. Raw and perfect. Too fast and way too slow.

"When I left I traveled the world." He gathers me to his heart. "I went to New York, Austria, Italy, France, Spain, and there are dozens more. But no matter where I went a piece of me was always here." His finger marks an X over my heart.

"I'm sorry I didn't tell you the truth. I wanted you to stay. But I get it now. I understand why you had to leave." I tilt my head back so I can see his eyes. "It just felt like having your dream meant I couldn't have you."

"Never." He kisses me. His chocolate kisses are sugar sweet and fill my insides with his warmth. "That's why

I'm glad you're coming to my office. I want you to see what I've built."

"Did you always plan to come back?"

"Always." I lean forward kissing him slowly. "Charlee, you'll be my wife one day. It can be now, next week, ten years from now. What do I have to do to keep you from running? From hiding behind that steel wall?"

"Give me time."

"You got it."

I kiss him as his eyes close.

"Love you, Darius."

"Not more than I love you." He says before drifting back to sleep.

I shake my head. This man is unbelievable. I curl up beneath him and hope I am as courageous as Darius. To see and get what I want. To keep pushing until my life is the life I dream about.

And for the first time, in a really long time, I let myself dream a little. Not about business or contracts but about a life with happiness, love, friends, and success. And somewhere in this dream of mine, I'd like to have my daddy back too.

CHAPTER 9

DARIUS

$\mathcal{I}$ slip from the bed before sunrise to shower and review emails. We got in a few hours ago, but I want to get to the office. I place my coffee on the nightstand.

I grab my phone to send a quick text to my mom. *GM! I'm back in San Francisco for a few days. I'll call you when I get back.* I place my phone back lowering to Charlee's side of the bed. She's nestled down under the covers.

I never thought I'd have her here, in my house, in my bed.

I weave my hand through the comforter. She's a wild sleeper. But last night must have worn her out because she didn't move an inch until I climbed out of bed. I kissed her, and she tucked the pillow under her head. She's laying on her stomach, so I brush my hands over her ass, giving it a squeeze.

I can't resist. I pull back the cover and replace my hand with a kiss. And crazy Charlee starts to wiggle.

"Trying to twerk on my face?" I chuckle.

"Nah, on your mustache." She says in her sexy morning voice.

"I'm down, turn over."

"Uh-uh…you nasty. I need to shower first." She laughs swatting my leg with a pillow.

"Oh, I'm nasty. All right…I see how nasty I am when I have you throwing it back tonight."

"Whatever!" She sits up, tossing the hair from her face. "Shit, I'd be all kinds of nasty to get a repeat of last night."

"Good morning Charlee Raine." I sit on the bed, leaning in to kiss her.

"Good morning to you too." She smiles. "Give me another one."

"Yes, ma'am."

I kiss her again. Our lips intertwine, and it feels like home and love. I can't believe I waited so long to have her again. My tongue fills her mouth, and she accepts pulling on my tie until we fall back on the bed. The kiss deepens as she sucks and nibbles as I reach around cupping both of her plump cheeks in my hands.

My phone chimes and Charlee pulls back. Her eyes search mine.

"What is it beautiful?" I settle between her thick thighs hating that I have to go into the office this morning.

"Your phone." Her head tips towards the sound.

"What about it?"

"Is there a line of women ready to cause drama?" Her voice is firm.

"The only woman in my life is my mom." I free a hand, reaching for my phone. I unlock it showing Charlee my mother's response, *Okay. Love you.*

"And me."

"What?" Now I'm confused.

She grabs my phone typing, then she passes it back with a kiss. "You have your mother and me."

I read the response, *Love you too.*

"And I'm the mess?" I say brushing against her heat. She shrugs matter-of-factly, and I laugh.

"If we are us, then that means we're the only people in this relationship." She says as if it needs clarification.

"You know that's not how I get down."

"People change." She wiggles to free herself, but I don't budge.

"You don't get say some shit like that and walk off Charlee." Her eyes won't meet mine. I turn her face to me. "If I'm with you, I'm with you."

"So how many women have you been with?"

"Get the fuck outta here. How many men have you been with?" She looks away. "Six years is a long time. You lived your life, I lived mine. All I know is we're here now."

She takes a deep breath. I spread quick kisses across

her face and down her neck. Then I nibble where she's ticklish.

"Stop!" She squeals.

I sit up. "So, while I'm gone, you can DM, text, or call whoever is waiting in the wings. Tell them you have a man now."

"Yes sir, *caveman*."

"I'm playing for keeps." I crawl out of bed removing my tie. I need to change my suit. I toss it in her direction. "So get your fine ass moving."

"Do I have time to shower and eat before we leave?"

"You don't have to go now. It's still early. I can come back and get you after lunch." I glance at the clock. That will give me at least five hours to work and tackle any significant issues first.

"Wasn't the point of me coming to see the office and see what you do?" She crosses her arms.

"Yes, but I don't want to bore you either. I have emails and phone calls and issues to address. Then I'm all yours." I remove my dress shirt, tossing it in the chair.

"Right."

"Don't say it like that. Here take my card. I'll have the car come around and take you wherever you want to go." I reach for my wallet, pulling out my card.

"That's not necessary." She pushes my hand away. "I'll be here when you get back."

"You're my guest. Take it Charlee." She stares at it. My mother's words enter my mind. She said I'd need to give her time. I drop to the bed gathering her to me. "Look,

don't fight me on this. I know you got your own money."
I roll my neck to make her laugh. "And you don't need a
man to tell you nothing." I give an exaggerated snap of
my finger. "But baby, I've waited my whole life for this.
Take it."

She takes the card.

"Do you remember that time we went to the mall?" I
ask as she stares at the card, running her fingers across
my name.

"Which time? We lived at the mall."

"That time we went into the Louis Vuitton shop." She
glances over her shoulder shaking her head. "You went in
to grab the latest purse, and I'd never been in that store
before. I knew the shit was mad expensive because it was
only ten items in the whole store."

She laughs. "Lies."

"What?! Those stores have lights and guards for three
handbags." I smile.

"Boy, you're a fool. Keep going." She leans back
against my chest.

"It was nothing really. You walked in, saw the bag,
dropped your daddy's card. And while we waited, you
walked around with your guys. I turned over the price
tag, and the purse cost $5,000."

"I don't even remember. It was probably another guilt
gift."

"A guilt gift?"

"Yes, that's our love language."

"What kind of psychobabble is that?"

"After my parents divorced my father started buying *things* to make up for the time. Purses, shoes, shopping sprees, trips, cars. Guilt gifts." Her voice cracks. "Finish your story."

"I will in a second. How are you handling the divorce and the new wives?" I don't want to ask about seeing her father and wife number three at church Sunday.

"I'm not. It's his life. I don't live with him, and I rarely see him. I figure if my mom has moved on so should I."

"Is that the way you want it?" I can't imagine having the opportunity to know my father. It's always been my mother and me.

"I'm still trying to decide." She fiddles with the sheet, pulling it across her body.

"Well, I'm here."

"I'll remember that. Now finish, or you'll blame me for being late to work."

She's right, it's almost eight. "$5,000 was like a million dollars to me. I promised myself that one day I'd take you shopping and drop my card on the table. I wanted to buy you nice things without checking the price tag."

"Well then here." She passes the card back. "I'll be here when you get back, and we'll go shopping together."

"You're amazing." I kiss the inside of her neck.

"Tell me about it."

I laugh, pulling her up from the bed. "We can do both."

"I'm good. Really." A sweet smile crosses her face. Her

eyes roam from my fade to my bare feet, taking in the state of my half-naked body.

"I need to change." I point towards the closet.

"Let me help you." Her smoldering gaze singes my skin. Her hands grip my waistband, bringing our bodies together.

She unbuttons my pants, letting them drop to the floor. My dick is rock hard and waiting.

"I think I remember how you like it." She teases wrapping her hands in a tight fist around my shaft. Pleasure tickles down my spine as she strokes me, then takes me into her mouth.

I groan gripping the back of her head. Her eyes find mine, as I watch her take all of me. She applies enough pressure twisting her mouth and hand up and down my shaft. My balls tighten, the sweet suction is too much. No woman has ever felt so good.

I try to pull out, but she grips her nails in my ass taking me deeper. My shit is tapping the back of her throat, and I can't hold back. A groan erupts from the depths of my soul as every muscle tense. My eyes find hers, my seed fills her mouth, and she drinks every drop.

I bring her mouth to mine, telling her how much I love her.

"Go Darius." She whispers across my mouth.

"Charlee...shit." My body is weak, and I want her in the worse way. "You trying to turn my ass out."

She pulls back and the shock filling her eyes is comical. "I can't with you."

"You don't have a choice. I have to go, but be ready for an all-nighter." I kiss her and smack her ass to hear her giggle.

"I'll be waiting."

I head to the closet floating. I've worked day and night for years, and suddenly life is going my way. "Love you, Charlee Raine," I yell from the closet.

"Hurry up before I come in there and jump your bones."

"I'm down with that kinky shit too." I toss back, gratitude fills me. I pause and look up at the Man. My life finally feels complete until all hell breaks loose.

CHAPTER 10

DARIUS

I'm bombarded with questions, meetings, calls. Delicious Chocolates deals with custom corporate edibles. We create custom molds to brand premier chocolate. This means partnering with brands on both sides of the transaction.

Most of our suppliers are international. I travel to find the best chocolate since I prefer to purchase from the source and build relationships. Then the VP, Shyann, handles clients. I rarely have to intervene.

Returning home, to Texas, was always part of my plan. Mainly due to my mother and Charlee, but also due to the lower cost of living, the affordable real estate, and I think a minority-owned brand can make a significant impact. But what I wasn't expecting is offers to remain in San Francisco.

I hear a knock at my door. "Come in."

"Glad to see you back." Shyann enters my office. I

stand giving her a hug. "You look refreshed. Austin was good to you." She brushes away a piece of lint off my jacket.

"Yes, it was." I sit on the edge of my desk. "What's this about a meeting with Mayor Ellis?"

"He's been a client for years, and he heard about our move. He is pushing to help us secure a permanent location here with perks."

I stand rounding my desk. "What type of perks?"

"He's in town. Want me to schedule it?"

"Yeah. Thanks."

She jumps up and heads out. Next is handling our Italian supplier.

Time flies. I catch up with Jack confirming our quarterly rate, then we plan to meet during my trip over the summer.

I grab some coffee. Now, with the fires out I jump back in reviewing contracts and returning calls. I've been away for almost two months. I'm floating from project to project. I stop to have lunch with the Mayor, followed by I meeting with our supervisor of production regarding our upcoming launch of holiday molds. Then I hear a knock.

"Yeah." I don't look up from my computer. We're having our best year yet. "What is it?"

"I need your keys."

"Charlee?" I glance at the doorway, and then the clock. It's after eight. I run a hand over my face. "I'm sorry baby."

"Look I get it. I went out to sightsee and realized I don't have a key. Thankfully the driver knew the address here."

"Why didn't you call?" I stand and walk over.

"I did."

Then I remember, I turned off my ringer during a conference call. "I think the ringer is still off. I had an international conference call. Let me grab it." I walk back to my desk. "Want to grab dinner?"

"No, I'm tired. It's been a long day. "

The tight set of her jaw says I'm in deep shit. I grab her shoulders turning her to me. "How pissed are you? On a scale from 1 to 10." She opens her mouth to respond, I kiss the inside of her neck. "And before you answer, remember, I love you."

She shakes her head.

"And, I'm taking you for a fabulous spa day, head to toe, on me."

She rolls her eyes.

"And, I know I'm your mother's favorite. So, she wouldn't approve of a level of piss-tivity beyond, I don't know, a four or five."

"Boy, you done lost your mind." She laughs, playfully hitting my chest.

"I'm sorry. I'll make it up to you."

"See this is why I can't fool with you. And when is my spa day?"

I freeze. "I'm not sure. I need to schedule it."

"You ain't slick Darius. Lying because you know you messed up."

"No, I was…." She caught me.

"Yeah, yeah, yeah. For the record, you can never ever tease me about being late. Never."

"Fine. I do have the best spa in town on speed dial." I wrap my arms around her with her back to my chest.

"Spas aren't open this late."

"For me, they will. What'll it be? A deep tissue massage, manicure, pedicure, facial." I feather kisses up the side of her neck. She smells good enough to eat.

"I recall someone mentioning an all-nighter." She turns over her shoulder, circling her arms around my neck.

"I got you!" I kiss her, hot and slow. I don't come up for air until we're both panting and ready for more.

She grabs my tie, lifting on her toes and retakes my mouth. I grip her ass in my hands, and her moans fill my office.

"I want you now," I tell her between kisses.

"Let's go, because you're not about to have me butt naked on a desk. I have to draw the line somewhere."

My woman has a way with words. I laugh running back to my desk to get my briefcase.

I lace my fingers with hers walking to the door when it swings open. Charlee gives me a *"Told you"* look.

"Oh, I'm sorry I didn't realize you had someone in here."

"We're just heading out. Charlee this is my VP Shyann."

Charlee extends her hand. "Hello, nice to meet you."

Shyann stares at Charlee's hand then up at me. "Charlee Stuart?"

I open my mouth to respond when Charlee jumps in. "That's correct."

"I apologize, I didn't mean to be rude. Shyann Lewis. Nice to meet you." I hear the tone change in her voice. I look at Shyann trying to figure out what just happened. Then I look at Charlee. They are engaging in a major stare down.

"Did you need something?" I ask.

"I was about to order take out." She held up the menus.

"Right," Charlee says turning to me. Her face is having an entire conversation. I'm obviously clueless because both of them are looking at me.

"No, I don't need to order anything because we are headed out."

"See you in the morning," Shyann adds.

"Yes, we will," Charlee responds.

Shyann leaves, and I turn to Charlee.

"What am I missing?"

"Your little girlfriend wasn't expecting to see me. I'll wait outside." Charlee stumps out.

My girlfriend? I glance back at the door. I turn off the lights following Charlee. I look down the hallway and see the lights in Shyann's office still on. I'll talk to her tomorrow.

I call a few favors before I slide into the car next to Charlee. I drape an arm behind her. In a blink, her hand is in my face. "I don't want to hear it."

We ride home in silence. She's watching the city ride past, I'm watching her. She's Level 10 pissed. The driver arrives at my house, and I open Charlee's door. She mumbles her thanks and walks to the door.

The driver whispers, "Good luck."

"I don't need luck, I need a miracle." He smiles as I pass him a tip. "See you in the morning."

I look at my woman at the door. I run up the stairs. I remove my keys, but before placing the key in the lock, I turn to Charlee.

"Can we squash this? I don't want to take this energy inside."

"You got it."

"Don't give me that fake agreement. I apologize for forgetting about lunch."

"And your girlfriend." Charlee faces me. She so hot I'm sure she'd spit flames if she could.

"Shyann is not my girlfriend. She's the VP of my company. We've never had a relationship other than friendship. Period."

"Right." She turns back to the door. *"Right"* is Charlee speak for her adding another guard outside her steel wall.

"Charlee..."

She looks at me. "It's squashed."

"Fine."

I open the door. There is nothing about this situation that feels handled. I replay the conversation over in my mind. What did Charlee see? Shyann and I have been friends since graduate school. She moved out to San Francisco when I told her of my plans to start Delicious Chocolates. I even told her about Charlee.

"I'll be back."

I hear Charlee mumble a response as I enter the master bedroom. Immediately I smell her scent. I remove my jacket and tie, tossing them aside. I drop to the edge of the bed to remove my shoes.

I hear the chime of my phone. I pull it out of my pocket.

How's it going? I smile as the bubbles dance on the screen. *Are you still at work?*

I could be better. I'm home. I remove the other shoe carrying them to the closet. *Why are you texting instead of calling?* I chuckle.

Because you have company. She adds a smiling emoji. *What happened?*

"Everything," I say. I can't tell her that because she'll call me then Charlee's mother. Then I recall my mother's words again, "You can't think you'll win her over with your looks or charm or money. That will not impress her."

I look towards the sound of the tv in the family room, unbuttoning my dress shirt. I go into the bathroom and run warm water in the jacuzzi tub. I run through a list of all the reasons I can't let this shit get to me.

I'm living in my dream home. I'm happy, in good health, I'm a strong Black man, and I'm rich.

I have my woman under my roof, and I refuse to let her remain pissed or to let myself ignore the apparent tension. This house is my sanctuary. Peace and love will abide here. Charlee and I will have to come to an understanding.

Now.

CHAPTER 11

CHARLEE

I flip through the channels. I don't usually watch tv, except for an occasional episode of crazy-ass Maury. There is something comical about his guest running off and rolling around backstage because the rooster came home to roost.

But as I sit here channel surfing, I feel like a Maury guest. I'm not pregnant and trying to decide who's my baby's daddy. But I'm feeling bird*ish*.

I want to run and roll around because life keeps fucking with me. I could call a car service and take my confused ass home. But even I would yell at my rich-girl ass problems to grow the fuck up.

I told Darius I wouldn't run and I'm willing to try at this relationship. But damn, did we have to jump into the deep in on the first day?

I teased Harper about wanting the Disney life, I guess

she's not the only one. Because what I know, is I love Darius, yet I'm letting fear fuck with me *again*.

So, instead of talking to my man, like a grown-ass woman, I'm channel surfing like a chicken shit. And I'm stuck in a city without my guys or my mother.

"That's some adulting for my ass." I drop back on the couch, tossing the remote aside.

"Come with me." Darius extends a hand. "Please."

"Why does your please have to sound so nasty?"

"Stop looking for something to bitch about. This is my fault. I apologize. I'm trying to show you that I fucked up. So, take my hand Charlee."

"Your apologies suck."

"Fine."

He scoops me up in his arms. I don't fight. I honestly don't have it in me because it seems like when I really fight, and fight hard, I lose. So, I do what I do best, I poke. "She was cute."

"Don't do that."

"And you never realized it, did you? How can men be so clueless?" I shake my head, mumbling the last part to myself. "She looked like her world crumbled around her, and you didn't even know." Much like my life, right now, if I wasn't cradled against his chest.

"Men are basic. Women are complicated. We say yes, we say no. Women say maybe to everything when in your heart you know exactly what you want when you want it, and how you want it done."

He has a point. Because despite being frustrated with myself for still being angry with him, I know I don't want to mess this up.

"I didn't see it because I don't go looking for trouble. I've known her since graduate school. And if you ask her, she's always known of my plans to win you back." He places me on the bed. "Lift your arms."

I follow his command, and I recall Shyann knowing my first and last name. He undresses me without a kiss or caress or tickle. Then I'm back in his arms again as if I weigh nothing. He carries me into the bathroom.

The vein at his temple is throbbing, which means he's furious. I want to hit rewind and start over. Then he lowers me into the bathtub. The water is perfect.

A ding dong rings through the air.

"I'll be back." He kisses my forehead and leaves.

I glance around. The lights are dim with candles around the room. I bite my lip to keep from getting emotional. It seems he remembers everything. We always shared bubble baths after an argument. We'd talk it out until we turned into raisins.

"I forgot this." He smiles adding a shower cap to my head. "Do you remember that time I messed up your sew-in trying to wash your hair?"

"Do I?" I chuckle.

He heads out again.

The bathtub is large enough to host a pool party. I braid my hair in two plaits and slip on the cap. Can't have myself looking like a chicken too. I laugh as the hot water loosens the tension in my body. I lay back, closing my eyes.

I guess this is where I have to boss up for real. It's not like I plan to step aside for another chick to have him. *That shit ain't happenin'*. And I promised to give us time.

A pop rings in the air. I jump opening my eyes. Darius is standing by a cart.

"I have wine, strawberries, ice cream, chocolate…" He points at each item, and I have to give it to him. He's trying.

"I'll take a glass of wine and the ice cream with a large spoon, please."

"Coming right up."

I place the wine on the side of the tub and scoop a hunk of the chunky ice cream. I groan from the pleasure happening on my tastebuds. "This is *sooooo* good."

"Scoot up."

I slide forward, and he sits behind me. His long legs extending on each side. Then he pulls me back to his chest.

"Talk." He says.

"I was at a Level 12, but now, after this ice cream, I'm at a Level 3." I take another spoonful, it's time I try too. "I guess I was jealous."

He sips his wine. "You guess?"

Our bathtub confessions meant we never had a knock-down-drag-out fight. Because face it, it's hard to remain pissed at a fine, naked man. With my chest to his back, I can process my thoughts without him reading my face, and I can let him speak his peace.

"I was." I lean back.

"Was?" He kisses my neck.

I shrug thankful this special time comes with a few unspoken rules.

We don't rush the processing time. We limit intimate touching because it can cloud our judgment. We don't leave the tub until it's all worked out. Lastly, we let the issues go like water down the drain once it's over.

Why I didn't insist on having a bathtub confession during our last big fall out? Because I knew he would stay.

The answer steals the last bit of fight, taking a sledgehammer to the steel wall around my heart. He teases me rightly. I have my shit on lock and key, and yet the silent tears fall.

I'm thankful my back is to him. I knew Darius would've stayed in Austin to be with me. I shovel ice cream into my mouth to keep from talking because he'll hear it in my voice.

Why? I whisper in my heart. Because I wanted to leave before he did. The wall falls and the gate swings wide open.

Fear did it to me again. Here I was mad at Darius, mad at men. I was playing the field, pointing fingers and acting a fool. I can't stop the shake of my shoulders, and my silent cry is a full out hot-ass mess.

"Baby, what is it?" He sits up, turning me to face him.

I can't answer. My soul is cleansing. This is the cry I've held back since I walked down the aisle at my father's wedding to his mistress.

CHAPTER 12

DARIUS

I've never seen Charlee like this. We had our bathtub confession, and suddenly she started crying. I lifted her from the bathtub and carried her to my bed. I cleaned up the ice cream, un-plaited her hair, and put on her pajamas. Then I crawled into bed beside her, holding her close and tight. I told her how much I loved her and that I'd always be here.

That was two days ago. She barely eats, and she won't let me in. I don't know how to fix it, but this shit is killing me.

"Baby please tell me what to do." I kiss the tender part of her neck that makes her smile.

"I'm okay." She whispers, but the smile never comes.

How is it possible to cry for two days straight? I reach for my phone to call my mother, then I know who can help. I find Charlee's phone and notice a group chat title "Guys."

Charlee's Angels. I thank God as I open the message and type, "SOS my Charlee Raine needs you. Plane on the way."

CHAPTER 13

I refuse to leave Charlee's side. So, I call the one person I know will help. But first I have to apologize.

I sit up in bed and reach for my cellphone. I call Shyann while keeping my eyes on Charlee.

"Hey, how's it going?" Her voice sounds distant.

"It could be better. Look I'll be out for the rest of the week. But I need to apologize and request your assistance."

"I'm listening."

I stand and adjust the covers around Charlee. I pace for a moment thinking about all that Charlee said.

"I apologize for using your feelings for me. It's recently come to my attention that I knew you had deeper feelings for me, but I chose to ignore it." I take a deep breath. Sitting in bed praying for my Charlee Raine to bounce back gave me time to consider the part I played. Whether it was six years ago or two days ago, I want to clean the slate and leave room only for her.

"I knew you still loved Charlee, I just thought I had a chance," Shyann says.

"I'm sorry if I ever sent mixed messages. We are a phenomenal team, but that's all we will ever be."

"I understand."

I hear the defeat in her voice, and I hate to be the cause of any pain. "You are an amazing VP. But if this somehow impacts your ability to remain with Delicious Chocolates, I'll do whatever is necessary to find a suitable alternative for you."

"I'd like that." She sniffles. "How can I assist you?"

I tell her about the incoming flight. She handles the hotel reservations and transportation for the guys while I remain by Charlee's side.

I can't believe the state of my life. I have to replace my VP, I still need to find a permanent location for Delicious Chocolates, I have billions in contracts that need my attention. But this king won't move without his queen.

CHAPTER 14

"Charlee, sweetie, wake up." I feel a slight shake. Now I know I'm dreaming.

I roll over ignoring the sound of Harper in my head. I pat on Darius' side of the bed. He must be in the bathroom.

I bounce around trying to find the perfect spot. Then I find a comfortable position. I hear snickering. He must've left the tv on.

"I see what's happening here. Darius gave her the *d,* and her ass is in a coma."

Is that Hunter?

"A dick comma? That sounds like something Charlee would have."

And Taylor.

"Probably had her screaming zaddy and tossing her dusty—"

"See that's why I can't stand y'all heifas."

Laughter fills the room. I open my eyes and look around. My eyes land on Hunter, Chase, Parker, Taylor, Payton, Alex, Ryann, Jordan, Taylor and Harper. All nine of my guys.

"Damn, and didn't none of y'all heifas put a lick of makeup on."

We laugh until we cry and this is the best kind of cry. My happy tears shift to sad ones when Harper gathers me in her arms.

"What are y'all doing here?" I ask.

"We got an SOS," Hunter says.

I lean forward and kiss my babies. "Hey, babies."

I let my head fall to Harper's shoulder. "Wait, I sent the SOS?"

"I did." Darius is standing in the doorway. A fresh wave of tears floods my eyes. "You needed them."

I scan the room again, and I did. I needed my guys, my sisters, and my man knew it.

"So Darius, you wouldn't happen to have a brother?" Chase bats her lashes.

"Nah, I'm an only child." He plays along, and the girls love it.

"A cousin…" Chase tries again.

"Or two…" Parker says.

"I'll see what I can find for you ladies, after breakfast." He motions to the front of the house, but his eyes are on me.

"Good, because I'm starving." Hunter jumps up, kisses my head, and waddles to the door.

"Charlee you have fifteen minutes to get yourself together." Harper kisses my cheek and follows the last guy out the door.

Darius crosses the room. I stand on weak legs, and he pulls me into his arms.

"I love you." I mean it, from the top of my head to the soles of my feet.

"Not more than I love you." He squeezes me tight.

"Thank you." I want to curl up inside his love and remain there.

"Ten minutes," Hunter yells.

"I need you to hurry and have these damn babies because I'm tired of you always trying to boss me around," I yell back.

"That's my girl." Darius laughs.

~

I shower and join the guys for breakfast. The spread is amazing. He told me about Shyann's help with getting the guys here. I called her, and we plan to get together for coffee. I look around the dining room table and spot an empty seat.

"I'll be in the office." He pulls me close for a peck on my lips, but I deepen the kiss. And I'm pleased when he doesn't hold back.

"Get a room!" One of the guys shouts.

"Mind your business." I toss back.

"Holler if you need me," Darius says before leaving us alone.

"That man is a keeper," Hunter says around a piece of bacon.

I walk around the table sitting in the vacant chair. Harper passes me a plate, and I dig in. I'm starving. I've been living on soup and juice. I feel their eyes on me, and I don't know where to begin.

"Thing 1 was my father's mistress."

There's a collective gasp. I don't address his wives by their names because their names are irrelevant.

"He told you?" Harper asks.

I shake my head taking a sip from my orange juice.

"Does he know you know?" Hunter asks.

I shrug. "We've never discussed it."

"How long have you known this?" Taylor asks.

"Since the beginning."

Harper grabs my hand beneath the table, and Hunter grabs the other. I call Darius back into the dining room. Then I slowly tell them about overhearing my father and Thing 1 on the phone while my parents were still married.

"Why did you agree to be a bridesmaid?" Hunter asks.

"My mother insisted that we take the high road."

"But she didn't know," Taylor asks.

"No, she didn't."

"And this is why you don't talk with your father?" Taylor asks.

"Yes."

Everyone is silent, I assume digesting this nasty lump of coal. I feel a gentle squeeze on my shoulders. I look up, and Darius kisses me so soft that my eyes water. "Love you." He whispers over my lips.

"Not more than I love you."

~

"I can't eat another bite." I drop the slice of pizza on an opened cardboard box and fall back on the love seat. The day was filled with food, laughter, and I feel human again.

Darius' family room is covered in blankets and guys. We're having a slumber party before they fly out in the morning.

"Are you better?" Hunter asks.

"Yes. Where would I be without you guys?" My heart is full too.

"I think you'd be a professional thot." Harper laughs. "She'd be throwing that thang around." I throw a pillow across the room, and it lands across her face.

"Liam must have the magic stick because you are feeling yourself," I add.

"Liam ain't the only one with a magic stick. *Aaaaahhhhh!*" Harper slaps high-fives the guys around her.

"She's on to something with that one." Taylor wags a thinking finger in the air.

"He did have you in a coma…" Hunter adds.

"And he got your weave all matted…" Chase says.

"And all blotchy and what-not…," Parker says pinching my cheek.

"Y'all sho know how to kick a bitch when she's down."

The chorus of our laughter is healing. I know I'll be all right. I have Darius and my guys. And I'm not ready to talk with my dad, I will soon, but only after I speak with my mother. I have to tell her everything.

For now, I'll enjoy my guys tonight and my man tomorrow.

CHAPTER 15

"*A*re you ready to head back?" I kiss the top of Charlee's head.

"Not yet." She waves as the sprinter pulls off with her angels. She spins around, "You don't mind, do you? I know you weren't planning on moving me in."

I place a finger over her sweet lips, and she runs her tongue up it, taking it seductively in her mouth.

"Stop it."

She wiggles her eyebrows.

"Stay as long as you want." I lead her back to the family room.

"What if I want to stay forever?" I pull her to my lap.

"I'd say, it's about time." I kiss her softly. I see the light in her eyes again. I owe the guys. "Let me see your phone."

Charlee reaches over and hands me her cellphone. I

find the group chat and message, *Send me the contract ASAP*.

The timeline fills with all types of party GIFs. I see dancing babies, Cardi B, Nene Leaks, even Snoop Dogg.

I turn the phone to face Charlee, and tears fill her eyes.

"Baby, if I see a tear I'm dead." He chuckles.

"Okay…okay…no tears." She's told me thank you a million times. I'm just glad she's better. "How can I help you?"

"Stick around for a while." I kiss her neck.

"Under one condition?"

I recall my words to her. "Can you believe it's been a week?"

"No more than I can believe we let six years pass without fixing our relationship." She lifts the hem of her shirt, then tosses it across the room. "Unfasten my bra."

I reach around her body, kissing the tops of her breasts. "Do you think this is wise?"

"Sit up." She leans back, and I follow her command. She removes my shirt, kissing across my chest. "Yes, Darius. It's wise and stop talking. Stand up."

"Yes, ma'am."

She undresses me. Her hands roam. Her tongue stops to sample and taste across my body, and I'm for it. I'm hoping it's not too soon but judging by the urgency in her eyes, she needs this. I need her.

She rakes her nails down my chest until they reach the waistband of my sweats. Heat feels my body and the rush of anticipation is not too far behind. Charlee is a head specialist. She'll have me screaming like a bitch and not giving a damn who hears me.

Our lips meet. I'm tonguing her down.

She pushes me back to the couch. Lightning strikes in her eyes. She climbs on my lap, brushing her sweetness against my wood. I run my hands up her smooth brown thighs, over her hips and palm her ass. Her moans fill the room because I have her tongue occupied.

She jerks back. "Are you clean?"

"Clean?" I snap.

"Yes, clean. I'm on the pill, and I want you skin to skin."

"Hell yeah." She shakes her head and laughs. "To both."

"Good."

She lowers on my dick, taking me in inch by inch until her wet heat wraps around my dick branding me. My eyes roll back in my head, and I hear a chorus singing.

"Baby your shit is tight." I hiss.

"I've been celibate."

My eyes snap open. "That's why you've been throwing that ass back."

"Shut your cocky-ass up." She's riding my dick like a certified cowgirl and still talking shit.

I buck with hard, deep strokes. Her head falls back, and I feast on her neck then her beautiful breast bouncing in my face. The moment I feel her wall flinch I turn it up.

I grip her shoulders driving us home like an animal. She's screaming and scratching. Her sounds feed my hunger to claim her, all of her.

Things are different between us. I know that she's all in, and I'm all in.

"You're mine Charlee Raine."

"And you're mine." Her words die becoming a deep moan.

Our passion fills the air until she screams in release and I do the same.

~

*C*harlee is asleep across my body. The couch serves as our bed. We've made love so many times I've lost count.

I brush her hair aside, leaning forward to kiss her lips. I fall back. *Is this a sample of our forever?*

She wiggles suggestively.

"You can't possibly want to go again." I tease.

"Not yet." She chuckles. "I'm cold."

I reach for a blanket from the floor, and I hold her tight.

"Mmhh, thank you." She snuggles against my heart and life is perfect. We have issues. I need to square away my business, she needs to get closure with her parents. But Charlee and I can handle it, all of it, I'm certain.

"Darius," she peaks out like a turtle. "I've been thinking."

"Oh hell…" I fold back the blanket.

"You haven't heard my proposal."

"Proposal?" Her lips are moving in slow motion like The Matrix, and my heart crawls to a stop.

"Don't look so petrified." She laughs. "Not that proposal."

"I'm not petrified, it's just when it's time I want to do the asking. Now, continue."

"Mind if I stick around? Really. I know Shyann is leaving and I can help around the office."

"You'd do that?" I know Charlee doesn't have to work. Regardless, of the drama with her father, he set her up for life.

"Sure."

"You don't have too, but I'd love to have you."

"Good." She stretches her neck to give me a kiss, then dips back beneath the cover.

"I guess that means we're exclusive." I tease.

She pops up again, "Hell yeah!"

"Then let's seal it with a kiss."

She crawls up my body, the kiss starts soft and sweet. Then escalates to a full-blown fire. I'm ready for round one thousand with the woman, and I hope it never ends.

"I love you." The sincerity in her eyes is like a shower of love.

"Not more than I love you, Charlee Raine."

Two years later...

I'm pumped. We are finally moving to Austin, thanks to Yuki Jameson. That girl knows how to come through like a champ. We've been bouncing back and forth between Austin and San Francisco. I'm now the VP of Delicious Chocolate and a real boss.

Before the plane lands, I'm gathering my stuff.

"What's the rush?" Darius asks.

"You know Harper is trying to one-up me. I have to get to the party before she does."

He laughs.

The twins are turning two. The party is today, and I can't wait for them to fall in love with their gifts.

"You guys are ridiculous."

"Laugh all you want. I will not be Auntie #2. I won't

have it." I'm acting extra, but I love my babies. "We seem to be multiplying like Gremlins."

"Tell me about it." He rubs on my stomach. Soon we'll add three more to the bunch, thanks to Harper and Liam expecting, Taylor and her mystery man, and my baby girl.

"Don't worry about the gifts I'll get them. But first, we need to stop by S&J." He says taking the packages from my hands.

"Fine, but make it quick."

"Yes, ma'am."

~

*W*e pull up outside S&J. The place is packed, as usual, judging by the parking lot. Yuki, Dylan's wife, meets us at the door.

It's baby season, because she's pregnant again. We hug turning our bellies to the side.

"Come on back." We follow, and I swear she looks like a young Kimora Lee Simmons. "I can't believe you can still fly."

"I don't have a choice. I miss home." I laugh. I'm four weeks from my due date. I turn towards the conference room.

"This way," Yuki says.

I look at Darius, as we follow and he shrugs. We cross the doorway, and my knees go week.

The courtyard is decorated, and I know the culprit. I turn to Darius. "What did you do?"

"From the moment I saw you, I loved you." Tears fill my eyes, but I can't look away. "Your sass, that ass," he whispers, and I hear laughter.

I glance over, and everyone in life that I love is here. My mother with her male friend. My father and his wife. She and I don't talk but I stopped calling her Thing 3, and that's progress.

I told my mother everything, and she understood why I kept it a secret, but my father is still in denial. I'm just thankful to have the burden off my shoulders.

"Baby what's going on?" I turn back.

"Can I finish?"

"Hurry up!" I shake my hands.

"Damn, a brotha gets no love."

"Lies!" I rub my belly, and the crowd laughs again.

Darius looks towards heaven. "Help me with this woman."

"I'm sorry." I bat my eyes. "I'm listening."

He clears his throat, and the humor leaves his eyes when he pulls out a box.

"I love you, all of you. Your beauty, your wit, your loyalty, your tenacity. The world is ours. And today, I'd like to make you my wife. Will you marry me?"

He peels open the lid. My hands cover my mouth, and I can't breathe or see through my tears.

He gathers me in his arms. "Is that a yes Charlee Raine?"

"Today?" I'm in shock.

"Yes."

I look around. "Right now?"

"Yes."

"What about the birthday party?"

"Woman." I hear the impatience in his voice.

"Sorry baby…" I smile. "Yes."

The crowd goes nuts. Then I hear music. He thought of everything. People are moving around, and I can't find my guys.

"Darius, I can't get married without my guys?"

"I know." A smile tugs at his luscious lips. "Hurry, the ceremony is about to start."

He hands me off to my father, and we turn towards the flower covered arch. The crowd sits, and a hat is lowered to my head. I turn around and see Hunter. She kisses my cheek, and that's when I lose it…again.

One by one, Taylor, Chase, Parker, Alex, Payton, Ryann, Jordan, and Harper each walk up hugging me and moving down the aisle towards Darius and his best man Zach Russell.

"Ready?"

"Yes, Daddy."

We start the walk down the cobblestone pathway to my man. Everyone is dressed casually, and I want to kiss Darius. I want to be his wife, but the thought of a wedding brings up bad memories. So, I guess this is our compromise. We're almost at the front, and I stop turning to my mother. I pull her to me and kiss her cheek.

"Love you Ma."

"Love you too baby."

I do the same to Miss Janice. And she can't hold back her tears.

"Thanks, Dad, I got it from here." I kiss his cheek. Then I walk the rest of the way to my man.

The rest of the ceremony is a blur except finding out the birthday party was a hoax. We eat at the food trucks and party all night.

Now, I'm sitting back with the guys. Darius is dancing with my mother.

"I think I need to break that party up." I tease, and the guys laugh.

"The Fine Wine Divas are trying to pounce on our men," Hunter adds.

"I wish they would. That man right there has a crazy wife." I point at Darius, and we laugh.

Mamma and her crew of first wives are dressed to kill. All eyes, young and old don't miss them. I reach for my drink and notice Taylor and Russell off in the corner.

"And what's that all about?" I whisper pointing across the way.

We all look over. Taylor yanks her hand walking at a ground eating pace into S&J and Russell is right on her heels.

"Oh shit."

"You think he's the baby's *daaddddeee*." I laugh.

"I say we go find out." Parker stands.

"I'm down," I say.

The guys stand and head towards the building.

"Charlee Raine…" I turn and see Darius. "Y'all go without me and tell me all the juicy details."

They go, and I'm pulled into my husband's arms. We dance and notice another lover's spat. "Look," I whisper.

"What?" His hand is spinning around.

"My dad."

Dad's eyes are locked on Mamma and her younger guys.

Darius laughs, "You think he has a shot?"

"Who?"

"Your daddy, that's who?"

I shake my head. "I'm not worried about him. It's my wedding day."

"Did I do good?"

"You did an excellent job." I kiss him. "This is perfect."

"Enough to bring the cowgirl out?" Passion fills his eyes.

"You ain't said nothing but a word." I lace his fingers through mine pulling him towards the building.

Darius pulls me back and kisses me tenderly. "Love you Charlee Raine Grant."

"Not more than I love you." I continue my stroll with an extra twist in my hips. He smacks my ass, and I throw my head back laughing.

"See that's how you got this one." I point at our bun in my oven.

"You damn right!"

I follow Darius out the courtyard and into our new life. Happy that I've found love again all thanks to his chocolate kisses and a hard-ass church pew.

AUTHOR'S NOTE

I said YES to a holiday romance writing project in 2019.

Ten authors. Ten holidays. Ten steamy romances. And we've all said yes to taking this journey together.

My ten stories are novella length. I think they're great for an evening of reading with your favorite glass of wine or tea. :) And I had the group of guys to make this series happen.

Then struts in Hunter and her squad, her guys. They came to me years ago. I love a good millionaire or billionaire romance like the next woman. But a few of my readers emailed me asking about a female millionaire. I thought why settle for one if I can write ten. **insert evil laugh**

I hope you enjoyed book one with Harper and Liam. Will you join me for the rest of the year as they build Platinum Prestige—one fly millionaire woman and hot guy at a time?

Don't miss a single release. Join my newsletter at **http://www.janesedixon.com/subscribe** to get updates and reader specials FIRST.

In closing, please leave a review. It helps others find my work and it keeps the lights on, if you know what I mean. ;)

I'll "see" you all soon.

Happy Reading,
Ja'Nese Dixon
www.janesedixon.com

P.S. Again, there are more Steamy Sensations Holiday Love stories available now. See them all on my website: http://www.janesedixon.com/steamy-sensations.

LEAVE A REVIEW

Did you enjoy *Exclusive Love*?

Please leave a book review **HERE**. Reviews are extremely important and it helps me continue sharing my books with fellow readers.

JOIN MY NEWSLETTER

Be the FIRST to know!

Consider joining my newsletter? http://www.janesedixon.com/subscribe Be the first to know about releases and specials. You can unsubscribe anytime.

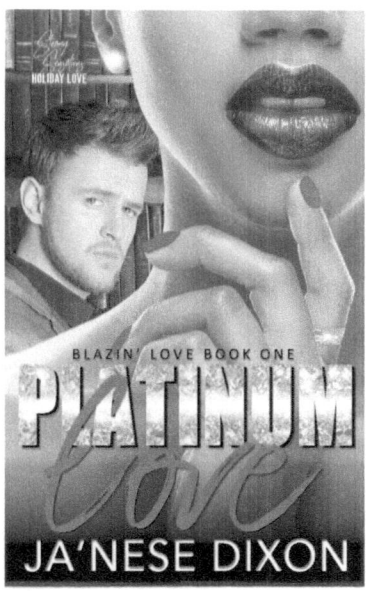

BLAZIN' LOVE BOOK ONE

PLATINUM
Love

JA'NESE DIXON

It's Valentine's Day.

I run to my favorite bar determined to figure out how I managed to lose my man and my inheritance in one night. The man is replaceable, but my monthly stipend is not.

I'm Hunter Preston. My friends call me Jo and I'm the only child to a media mogul. I was traveling the world, living my best life, until Daddy dropped a million-dollar bomb, annihilating my boujee world.

Double or nothing.

He gave me thirty days to pitch a million dollar business concept, or I can say goodbye to my trust fund.

So, here I am with my girls, trying to get more than selfie advice, when Ben, the sexy bartender—who either abhors me or he's immune to my flirting—offers to help write the business plan under one condition. He wants $50,000.

$50k to get $1 mil sounds reasonable until I remember how hot he is and how off-limits he is and how he wants nothing to do with a woman like me.

I'm screwed, pass me another drink.

Get Your Copy on Amazon
or Read in Kindle Unlimited!

Read an excerpt on www.janesedixon.com.

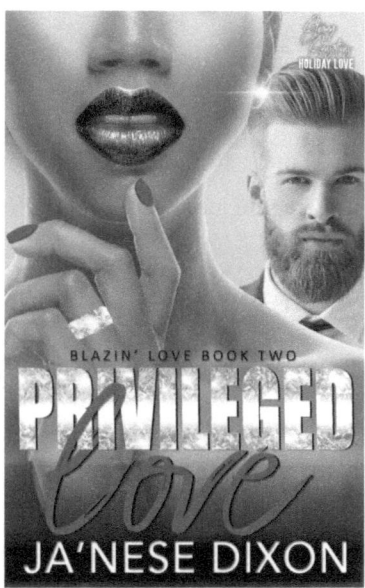

It's St. Patrick's Day.

The day is really not important, at least that's what I thought. I dress to impress, ready to secure my first contract as a partner with Platinum Prestige.

Simple, right? No, I wish.

I'm Harper Price. I've joined my best friends in starting an elite concierge service and I'm up. My sole task is to lease an airplane from Liam.

I walk in, he proposes, I walk out.

Apparently, his billionaire have gone to his head and now the sexy, arrogant menace won't leave me alone. His head is hard as a brick. (Take that any way you want.) And he refuses to accept "no" in any language. But I'm done with love.

No more.

Nada.

No mas.

Yet secretly, I'm scribbling my first name with his last name. Then he whispers, "Live a little Harper." And his money green eyes shine like dollars signs as he throws an unexpected curve ball. He'll grant three wishes, when…not if…I say yes.

Does having the most eligible rich bachelor begging to put a ring on it make me lucky? Hell no!

Not when my heart is screaming leap, my head is screaming caution, and my panties are.…

Oh hell, this is a f'in plane crash waiting to happen.

What is a woman to do?

Get Your Copy on Amazon
or Read in Kindle Unlimited!

Read an excerpt on www.janesedixon.com.

COMING SOON

ELEGANT LOVE

JOIN THE NOTIFICATION SQUAD!

Are you loving the guys of Platinum Prestige? Don't miss *Elegant Love*, Book 4 in the *Blazin' Love* series. Join the notification squad.

Get the Alert!

**Millions of adoring fans dream of having one
night with him, but only she has access to his
heart.**

Born with three commas in his bank account and
melodies in his veins, Marques Carter is the rising
prince of R&B. But not even his family name can
guarantees success.

Brione Allen is a smart woman that made a
dumb decision: trusting the wrong man. He
blackmailed her family and now she's bound by a
debt they knew she couldn't pay.

A chance meeting at his concert leads to an
encrypted proposal: One week, one hundred
thousand dollars, one incriminating secret. But
when extortion and family ties expose them to the
worst of the limelight, which secrets will they

keep…and which will threaten their small light of hope?

**Get Your Copy on Amazon
or Read in Kindle Unlimited!**

*T*he same time every week for three years and the call got no easier. Brione Allen sat on the couch and blew out a deep breath. Dial the number. Ask for Kayla. But the knot in her stomach told the utter truth. Nothing about this was easy for her.

She tapped the numbers by memory, adding it to her favorites was something she couldn't stomach, not after all they'd done to her.

"Hello."

"Good evening Mrs. Bradley is Kayla around?" She stopped asking to speak with her hoping to gain a sense of control in the situation, but they held her captive with a vice grip on her heart.

"Hello to you too Brione." Her dusty voice held an air of censorship. "I'll call for her."

Kayla had a nanny, private school, and just about everything a little girl could want.

"Brione." She cringed at hearing his voice.

"Stewart, I was holding for Kayla."

"She'll have to call you back."

"But today is my—"

"Talk to you later."

The line disconnected and Brione screamed. No one heard her, and no one cared. Alone in her fancy plush prison, she'd gladly trade for their freedom.

She fell back on the couch and stared at the ceiling fan and her cellphone rang. She popped up anticipating the sweet sound of Kayla's voice. But the screen displayed another welcomed caller.

"Eliana Marshall. To what do I owe this honor?" Laughter flowed through the phone, Eliana was the only person she let close. The only person she trusted. The only person who knew the truth.

"Let's see…I'm your best friend. So I need no reason to call other than to hear your wonderful voice." Brione smiled. "Second, I'm flying into town, and I refuse any excuse you make for not seeing me."

Brione gripped the phone to her ear as she toyed with the hem of her blouse. She'd rushed home from work for nothing.

"I apologized a million times. But you plan to milk it dry," she joked pulling her stocking covered feet beneath her body and relaxed.

"I plan to milk it until it turns to powder if that will get your butt out of that condo. I will *not* take no for an answer."

"Milk it dry *and* add in a level of guilt to the recipe."

"You got it." They laughed. "How are you?"

"I've been better." Brione looked around the room, furnished with the finest, reeking of their wealth. "You're heading here for the weekend?"

"No, I'm heading back indefinitely. Bruce and his wife are expecting twins, and they're keeping a close watch on her. We're planning to hang out in Houston until the babies arrive. Her doctor and family are all there. So, it could be a couple of months or longer."

"Yay!" Brione sat up, excited. "It will be nice to have you in town for a while."

"Just know I plan to pop up on your doorstep and drag you to a party or two while I'm there." Brione shook her head knowing they would have a battle ahead.

"How are you enjoying your job?"

Brione listened as Eliana shared her love of working for Bruce Daniels. She bounced around from Atlanta to Houston and back as his assistant.

"I can't believe the luck I've had with getting this job. It is stressful but fun. I'll be assisting Marques for a while too."

"Who is that?" The name sounded familiar, in a fuzzy, vague way.

"What rock do you live under?"

"The law school rock." She snickered. "I don't have time for anything but class and studying. Well, that and my side gig."

"Side gig?"

"Eliana, who is Marques?"

"Oh, yeah. How do you *not* know who he is?" Her amazement was evident by the squeak in her voice. "He's a caramel dipped...tall, muscled...*god* in living color."

Brione lifted a brow at Eliana's description. "All that?"

"Yes, he's the epitome of sexy. Too bad he's my boss." She let out a sigh. "Anyway, he's an R&B singer from Atlanta. I guess you wouldn't know him since he's more underground." She was all business. "He is the flagship artist of Rockstar Entertainment. We're preparing to release an EP then his debut album."

Brione tried to picture this caramel sexy god. Her failed attempt morphed into her last dalliance that turned her life upside down, inside out, and left Brione estranged from her family.

"That sounds like a lot of work." Brione didn't listen to the radio and rarely watched TV. Her sights were set on securing an associate's position with a major law firm. Fun took a backseat.

"It is, which is part of the reason for my call." Eliana said.

"Oh, it wasn't just to hear my wonderful voice?"

"Of course."

"Yeah, yeah, yeah. Spill it, Honey." Brione walked to the kitchen and opened the freezer, pushing around the contents until she found the frozen lasagna.

"Do you still help with events?"

"Yes, what's up?" She peeled back the corner of the lid

and popped the plastic bowl into the microwave. Then she leaned a hip against the counter.

"Bruce's anticipated maternity leave and Marques' EP has opened a lot of doors for me. They've asked me to oversee the launch with hopes of promoting me to A&R."

"Congrats!"

"Thanks, but hold it for now. I still need to get through this project."

"So, basically it's an interview."

"Exactly."

"How can I help?" Brione dropped her head and chuckled at the faint sounds of Eliana's clapping. Eliana could make it happen without her, but Brione wanted to see her friend succeed. "I didn't say yes yet."

"But you will." Eliana blew a kiss through the phone. "I want to host a release party in Houston, and I'd love to bring you in. It pays good, and I'm almost certain I can get you the gig."

"Really? But I've never done a music event."

"Don't worry about that. Your work is impeccable, you're organized, timely, and you work well under extreme pressure. Are you free Saturday?"

"Yes, how about ten?"

"That's perfect. Get together your portfolio and let's meet at the cafe on Saturday. I'll try to get either Bruce or Marques there too. That way I can cross two tasks off my list at once."

"I like the sound of that."

"You would, Miss Planner Chic. I maintain, where you thrive. One day, I'll grow up to be just like you."

Brione shook her head as if Eliana could see her. "No, ma'am. Grow up to be like you, and you'll be just fine."

"The thought of peanut butter and honey back in business is enticing don't you think."

"Houston ain't ready for us," Brione added.

Eliana's robust laughter rang through the phone. "Girl, if only they knew! And for totally selfish reasons, it would be a lifesaver to have your help *and* get to spend time with you without you skipping out on me."

They haven't seen each other in years, for one reason or another. But Brione missed her too. "I got you. When we're done, they're going to beg you to take that position. And I'll be there at 9:45 ready to rock n' roll."

"Awesome. I'll text you if anything changes. I gotta go, we're about to land." Eliana said.

"Be safe." The microwave beeped.

"I will. Love you Peanut Butter." Eliana giggled.

"Love you too Honey." They disconnected, Brione stood staring at the phone for a minute considering their long friendship.

Eliana was her roommate in college, their running nicknames came when all they could afford was Ramen noodles, and peanut butter and jelly, except Eliana, liked hers with honey or syrup.

Music was Eliana's passion like organizing events was Brione's. However, she knew her love of centerpieces and tulle could not lead to her desired destination.

Brione gathered her hot food from the microwave and walked to the dining room, she turned into an office. She stared at the stack of textbooks. She entered law school for two reasons: money and time. The family connections between the Bradleys and her parents guaranteed her seat. But her high GPA landed her a full ride.

She cleared a space for her bowl, tonight she'd study and tomorrow she'd order pizza and work on her portfolio. She lowered into the chair in front of her laptop, placing her food aside. She opened the oversized law book and turned to the cases she needed to read and analyze for class tomorrow.

She leaned over the keyboard and forked a chunk of lasagna, she cradled her hand beneath it to keep the sauce from dripping onto her expensive textbooks. She popped it into her mouth and did a chair dance as the ricotta cheese and Italian sausage made her taste buds happy, momentarily overlooking that it almost burnt her tongue. She pushed the bowl back to let it cool and read the first legal case when her phone rang again. The little face on the screen made her heart race with joy.

"Hello, Sweet Pea." Her voice trembled, she took a deep breath.

"Hi!" Brione could envision her chubby cheeks, full eye lashes, and radiant smile.

"I think this is the best surprise I've had all day." Her giggle warmed Brione's heart. "How was school today?"

Kayla talked about crayons and finger painting. Her

new best friend and a boy pulling her pigtails. All the things Brione had to experience by phone and not in person. And as soon as the call started it ended, sending exaggerated kisses through the phone to the tune of Kayla's sweet laughter with promises of talking with her again on Saturday.

Life wasn't fair. That was too tall of an order.

Brione used the fork to cut into the cooler lasagna. She had stopped crying about it and questioning why long ago, instead she dealt with it, taking blow by blow and somehow managing to bounce back. But tonight she wanted to sit in it. From the sting of the scheduled phone calls to Stewart consistently dangling their freedom like cheese enticing a rat, reminding herself that she had a plan. This ache in her chest was only temporary.

One day she and Kayla would live under the same roof. Holding on to this goal kept her in one piece.

Kayla motivated Brione to work hard and she vowed not to repeat the same mistake twice. Men like the dreamy caramel sex god Eliana drooled over were bad news. Stewart was one of them. He walked into a room and every woman—married, single, it didn't matter— wanted him. She'd thought herself lucky.

Brione snickered at her foolish youth. None of them cared about what she wanted in life. Her goals. Her desires. To the Bradleys, her parents, Stewart, she was their pawn, their minion, their tool. *So they thought.*

She couldn't afford to crack. She ate the rest of her

dinner, deciding to study first then get her portfolio together for her meeting with Eliana.

To get Kayla back, she needed money and landing the job with Eliana to organize Marques' event could be the break she'd prayed for.

Walking into Coffee Confessions had a ring of a homecoming for Marques Carter. He had spent many days hanging around waiting on Bruce to finish a shift before they went to the studio. Houston saved him and got his life back on course. Now that he was back, he hoped lightning would strike again for them.

He pulled the baseball cap lower to disguise himself. The release of his first official video last week gave him more than his usual double takes. In Atlanta, he couldn't go anywhere without people recognizing him, here offered a reprieve. But he didn't want to take any chances, welcoming the way people bumped right past him. It added another reason he loved being back in Houston.

Marques arrived early to meet with Bruce. He scanned the room, spotting a few empty tables and made his way to the line. He lifted his head to read the menu when he felt a soft bump behind him. He turned around and had to glance down at a petite woman.

"Excuse me." She held up a hand then reached out to stabilize a mug rocking back and forth on the shelf. "I was trying to miss the stroller and then the display and…" Her voice stalled as she finally looked up at him. Her lips parted in surprise. "Huh, sorry."

He chuckled. "I think I'll live."

She nodded without speaking as their gazes held. Marques let his eyes survey her light brown skin paired with jet black hair. It was curled softly brushing the sides of her face in a chic bob. Her heart-shaped face and doe eyes held curiosity as her full lashes brushed her high cheekbones with each exaggerated blink behind black frames. But when he zeroed in on her full lips coated with a hint of gloss, her tongue darted out and a groan reached his ears. He didn't know if it came from him or her.

"Andrew Carter." Using his legal name seemed appropriate as he extended a hand ready to see if her skin was as soft as it appeared.

"Brione Allen." Her smooth husky tone reminded him of a midnight radio jockey. The type of voice that held intrigue, mystery, and allure.

She accepted his hand and lightning passed from her touch through his body. *Damn.* Her eyes flashed to meet his as his heart rate tripled. He studied her thoughtfully, appreciating the heat lingering in the depths of her brown eyes.

"Welcome to Coffee Confessions, give in to your guilty pleasure. How can I be of service?" The barista behind the counter asked and Marques was at a loss for words. He still held her delicate hand in his thinking Miss Brione Allen was a guilty pleasure he'd gladly give in to. But judging by the penetrating stare she gave him as she snatched her hand away from his, he doubted she was on the menu.

"I'm sorry, I need a moment to review the menu. Brione after you." He extended his hand towards the counter and she stepped forward. She appeared as surprised as he was. The chemistry between them was as real as the nose on his face.

"Huh, sure." She stepped to the counter and tossed her purse on her shoulder like a barrier between them. *No, baby girl, that purse ain't gonna save you.*

She started to order and the sounds of the room faded into oblivion as Marques scanned the length of her body, the curve of her backside, and...

"And for you sir?" The barista wiggled his eyebrows. Heat rose to Marques' face, *caught*. But her hips were too tempting to ignore in pants that left no curve to the imagination.

"Our order is not tog—"

"Make it two of what she's having." He passed his credit card and turned back to Brione.

"That's not necessary."

"You're welcome," he teased, her expression much too severe for him.

Her eyes softened, "Thank you."

Brione stepped to the side and waited as Marques collected his receipt. They stood in heated silence both snagging discreet glances at the other waiting for their coffee. He had no clue what she ordered, thankfully he wasn't allergic to anything.

His senses were ablaze with her nearness. The closest comparison would be the moment he completed a new song. It gave the dueling emotions of exhilaration and exhaustion simultaneously.

"Are you off to work today?" He noticed the button up blouse and dress slacks.

"No, I'm meeting a friend. And you?"

"Business." She scanned his body in a sweeping motion. He wore a baseball cap with jeans and shirt. His goal was to blend in with the good people of Houston. He wished now that he'd given it more thought. Her mouth took on an unpleasant twist. "What you don't approve of my casual attire?"

"Oh no. I think it must be nice."

He searched her eyes and wished he could read her mind. The barista called his name for the order. Marques passed a cup to her and grabbed his own. The place was filling up quickly. He snagged a table and pulled out a chair for her.

"Join me while you wait." She hesitated. "Please." Brione slowly lowered to the chair. The floral scent of her perfume couldn't compete with the aroma of the coffee beans but it was a soft statement of her presence in the busy cafe.

Marques sat across from her finding it hard to contain the odd sensation in the pit of his stomach. He took a drink of the hot coffee to distract himself. The taste of caramel and whipped cream warmed his mouth. "This is delicious. What is it?"

"A custom drink. It's my favorite." She lifted the cup to her mouth and took a sip too. Remnants of her gloss left on the white lid.

"I'll have to get this again." He grabbed his phone and snapped a picture of the sleeve. "So Brione tell me, are you from Houston?"

She sat her cup on the table, pulling closer. Their knees brushed, her eyes widened. "No."

He waited for her to continue, she crossed her hands over the table. "Are you always this talkative?"

Her husky laughter rippled through the air. "No, it takes me a minute to warm up to people."

He nodded. Brione dropped her hands to her lap, "What about you? Are you from here?"

"No, I'm from Georgia."

"You said you're here on business. What type of business are you in?"

"I'm in a family business. I'm taking a little time off before we enter a busy season." It was obvious she didn't recognize him. It made him relax, he didn't feel "on."

"Do you travel often?" She asked.

"Not as often as I'd like."

"So you enjoy traveling?"

He nodded, "I do. It is a love of mine, I acquired it as a child. I traveled a lot with my parents." He took a drink of his coffee. He joined his father on many tours over the years. "The food, architecture, music, museums, I love all of it."

"Where all have you visited?" The warmth of her smile echoed in her voice.

He crossed his arms over his chest and extended his legs. "I visited, at last count, 40 or so of the great states of America. I've hit the tourist spots. Australia, Canada, South Africa, Rome, London, Egypt, I love it there too. Dubai, New Zealand, India, China, Morocco, Italy, Bali. There are more but you put me on the spot."

"Tell me about your favorite place." She leaned over the table and rested her chin in her hand. Her eyes bright and inquisitive.

"Uh…" her smile made it hard to think straight, he searched his mind, "I can't pick just one. My most recent trip was to Bora Bora."

"That place is on my wish list." A smile danced on her lips, heat coursed through his veins. *Get a grip!*

"Put a star by it. It is a place you'll never forget. The warmth of the water. Its vibrant turquoise color. There's something magical and healing about the island."

Her expression stilled and grew serious.

"Add this one to your wish list too." He wanted to see her smile again. "Torres del Paine National Park."

The spark returned. "Where is that?"

Marques leaned forward enjoying the light in her eyes. "It's in Chile. There's more sheep than people but the valleys are the most vibrant green and the sky the bluest blue you'll ever see. There is a small window when the weather is appropriate but it is worth it." He winked and something told him she mentally noted every word.

He wondered what she was thinking as she dropped her head, brushing her hair behind her ears. Her phone buzzed against the table and Brione glanced down at the screen.

"That's my friend." She held up her phone and finished her coffee. "We have to reschedule."

She stood from the table and leaned over to toss the empty cup in the trash.

"Would you like another?"

"No, I have studying to do."

"Studying?" He hoped to prolong her departure.

"I'm a law student." The glimmer in her eyes dulled.

"If I remember correctly there are three of them here."

"You are absolutely correct." She placed her purse on her shoulder and picked up a black portfolio. He missed that earlier.

"Would you like to grab lunch or something?"

"I really need to go." She shook her head and glanced at her phone. "Thank you for the coffee and the conversation." An easy smiled played at the corners of her mouth.

"No, thank you for this wonderful concoction." He held up the cup shaking it.

"You're welcome. Have a nice day." She turned to leave and he reached for her arm.

"Take my number. I'm in town for a couple weeks. I *really* would like to see you again."

"I don't have time. I—"

"Take it…just in case. Pass me your phone and I'll enter it."

She searched his eyes for so long he thought she'd say no again.

"Okay." She hesitantly passed her unlocked phone, holding the top with the tip of her fingers, as if trying to avoid his touch.

He entered his personal cellphone number and placed the phone in her open palm. "I'll talk with you soon."

*B*rione sat to study for finals, she had two weeks left before summer break. But his voice, his smile barraged her. "Study Bri!"

Thoughts of coffee with Andrew had her head in the clouds. The way his head fell back when he laughed. The twinkle in his eyes when he teased her. It was a chasm in time that passed too fast, she wanted more.

Closing her eyes she estimated his height was close to six feet, the outlines of his shoulders strained against the fabric of his shirt. He stood before her with his hands shoved in his pockets and a killer smile wide with perfect white teeth. His classically handsome features made him beautiful for a man.

People passed their table slowing to gawk at him, not once did he look away or acknowledge their presence. She wondered what his hair looked like beneath the cap but figured it really didn't matter. The man could be bald and she was sure she'd find him absolutely breathtaking —star quality.

Brione shook her head trying to rattle the images of him from her memories. But it proved impossible.

She tried reading the case at least ten times with no luck. But his soft encouragement, add this one to your wish list, rendered it impossible. Adding him to her list sound better. *Forget it.*

She opened her laptop and clicked on an internet browser. She typed in, Torres del Paine National Park and pressed enter. The results populated, her inner child didn't know where to start. She squealed stomping her feet beneath the table to release the energy. Pictures, she'd start there.

Brione clicked on "Images." The pictures before her eyes made her lean into the monitor. There were mountains, valleys, glaciers, snow, a winter heaven. What had he done during his visit? Did he hike? Was he alone? Was it as cold as it appeared?

She grabbed her phone and went back to his contact. And she noticed the note, Call me and let's have dinner sometime. She had stared at it for most of her *non-effective* study time.

She could send a text.

Her fingers hovered over the screen. No. She shook her head, and then what? He'd text her back and want to talk on the phone. She put the phone back on the table. Music. That would help.

She stood and turned on the wireless speaker,

stopping by the kitchen for some water. Back at the coffee table, she sat in front of her textbook. She untwisted the top off the plastic bottle and took a cool drink. She scanned her phone for some music, pressed play and turned back to the case.

Brione read through several immigration cases for class. Her doorbell rang and she glanced at the clock. She wasn't expecting anyone, she never had guests except... She stood up and walked to the door and glanced through the peephole. Her heart dropped to her feet. *What is he doing here?*

Stewart leaned into the doorbell. *Ding dong. Ding dong. Ding dong.*

"I know you're there. Open up and stop staring at me through the peephole."

Brione jerked back, placing her back against the door. She cracked her knuckles and exhaled a shaky breath. Her palms sweaty, she looked down at her t-shirt and leggings. Her clothes didn't matter. But she felt more in control in a suit. Less like the young woman that fell for his smile and honey-laced words only to get stung by a wasp.

"You can do this Bri," she whispered running her wet hands down her pants. She clutched one hand in the other to still her shaking limbs. "This is your space. You are in control."

Ding dong. Ding dong. Ding dong.

"I'm not leaving." He stated.

She placed a hand on the handle and unlocked the

bolt. She peeked through the opening created by the chain. "What do you want?"

"I promise this is not the way you want to handle this situation." He leveled his deadly stare.

"I'm studying."

"I guess Kayla will call you next week then. Give you time to study." He stepped back never breaking eye contact with her. She unlatched the chain, stepping back as he strolled in like he owned the place.

Brione closed the door. Stewart was like the boogeyman. People refute its existence until it pops up under your bed.

He sat on the couch and leaned back. "Are you always this rude to your guests?" He stretched his arms across the cushions, obviously comfortable. "Can I get some water, sweet tea, a sandwich? Damn." He laughed at his own joke.

"You didn't drive to Houston for water or a sandwich. So stop with the dramatics. What do you want?"

"What I've always wanted, *you.*"

Stewart Bradley knew how to pop up on her doorstep when she felt confident, when she finally decided to not let him push her around, then he emerged from the shadows to call her bluff.

"Have a seat? I won't bite."

The invisible shackles clanked around her ankles as she sat in the chair closest to the door. "What do you want Stewart?"

"How are you?" His eyes scanned her body. She

wrapped her arms protectively around her waist.

"I'm fine."

"When did you cut your hair and what's up with your clothes?"

"Stewart I'm studying." His mother was always dressed to perfection including a string of white pearls. He wanted a clone of Mrs. Bradley, the thought of her old sweats and short hair irking him brought a smile to her face. "And I like my bob."

"Is this how you're carrying yourself nowadays?"

"Is that why you visited? If so, we can end this conversation here and now." She swallowed hard.

"Don't let law school go to your head. This is still my show."

"Why don't you move on and let us move on too?

"There is no *us* without me," he growled. "You got into law school because of me. You can't care for Kayla without a job. What about her education? Her tutors? Her nanny? And don't forget about your pops." His glare intimidating. "I will deliver his career in a wastebasket. Is that what you want? Do you want to ruin everyone's lives because of your selfishness?"

The boogeyman live and in living color. Panic was rioting inside her gnawing away at her confidence. Gnawing away at her plans and dousing her hope.

She once trusted this man and thought he loved her. That was the face of love. It was laughable. Her tongue felt thick and her nerves made it hard to form a coherent thought. She was tired of him pushing her around.

Don't let him push you around. Brione couldn't trust that voice, hadn't she invited him into her life in the first place. She dropped her head, stirring uneasily in the chair, hoping to hide the shame from his probing eyes. It was the cost of trusting an untrustworthy person. A person who valued self-ambition and greed over people. *How had I missed it?*

"Are you done playing with me?" His nostrils flared with fury.

She nodded, fear splintered her heart.

"Good." The storm clouds left his eyes. "Mom wants us to set a date."

She squeezed her eyes shut gripping the arms of the chair. "Stewart you don't want to marry me. We have nothing in common—"

"Nothing in common? We have *everything* in common. Let me shoot it to you straight. I want a date or so help me, Brione Allen, I'll bury you and your father's dreams of sitting in the Oval Office. And I'll ensure you never ever see our daughter again." He ground the words out through clenched teeth. "Understand?"

"Yes."

∾

Continue Reading...

**Get Your Copy on Amazon
or Read in Kindle Unlimited!**

Hidden Desire (Book 3)

Ready for Love Boxed Set (Books 1 - 3)

Smith Pact Duo (Contemporary Romance)

Yuki's Luck (Book 1)

Tempting Asher (Book 2)

Smith Surprise (Book 3)

See all of my books on my website:

http://www.janesedixon.com/books.

Steamy Sensations
HOLIDAY LOVE

10 Authors. 10 Holidays. 10 *Steamy Romances*.

Ten romance authors bring you a sexy story to fire up your holiday. Each author has their own series in 2019 with one thing in common - Holidays!

Check out all of the Steamy Sensations books HERE or my website janesedixon.com/steamy-sensations!

ABOUT THE AUTHOR

Ja'Nese Dixon pens tales of romance in several sub-genres. But her favorites are the ones that manage to keep readers sitting on the edge of their seats lying to themselves about reading "just one more chapter".

Ja'Nese is an avid reader and coffee drinker, who also loves to run, cook, and craft. Her ultimate goal as a writer is to give you a little "staycation" with every story. And she aims to make this present story no exception. Sit back, grab a snack and enjoy.

Ja'Nese calls Houston home with her husband, three kiddos and a four-legged diva dog.

Visit her website at www.janesedixon.com if you enjoy romance, suspense and good stories.

Subscribe to Ja'Nese Newsletter "Reader's Staycation" for reader exclusives, regular giveaways and more.

Stay in Touch:
www.janesedixon.com
info@janesedixon.com

facebook.com/AuthorJaNeseDixon

twitter.com/janesedixon

instagram.com/authorjanesedixon

amazon.com/author/janesedixon

bookbub.com/authors/ja-nese-dixon

ABOUT THE PUBLISHER

Purpose Prevails Publishing
2231B Center St. STE 144
Deer Park, TX 77536
www.purposeprevailspublishing.com